ABOUT THE AUTHOR

Kenechi lives in London and enjoys writing fantasy fiction, romance and short stories (some of which she posts on her blog). She also hates the cold and hopes to one day figure out how to hibernate in winter.

D144Ø6Ø6

Aversion

Book One of The Mentalist Series

KENECHI UDOGU

Aversion

Book One of The Mentalist Series

OTHER BOOKS BY KENECHI UDOGU

The Other Slipper
The Altercation of Vira
The Summer of Brian

ACKNOWLEDGMENTS

I would like to say a massive thank you to my family and friends for acting as my lab rats all through the many stages of the writing of this book. Okey, Neso, Chioma, Chizoba, Ethan, Rob, Pi-Lin, Dumebi – you guys are the best.

My beta readers were amazing with all their input and insight so I'd like to extend my appreciation to Annabelle Marie Veronica, Fara Hanani, Ruty Benitez, Martha Campos and Nat Mercado for all their support. Double thanks to Fara for all the additional help she provided in tying up the loose ends before the book launch (you know what I mean - thank you, thank you, thank you). I would also like to acknowledge Abona Frost for being so patient with me and providing the lovely design that graces the cover of this book. Many thanks to Rebecca Sauve for getting involved with this project.

And last but not least, I'd like to thank my wonderful parents for never freaking out at my eccentricities.

ONE

My name is Gemma Green and I am an Averter. You're probably wondering what that means and why it is important for me to state that I am one. On the surface there is not much difference between me and most other fifteen year old girls, except for the fact that I have the ability to alter people's minds and stop them from carrying out actions that will unhinge their predestined life paths. I know it sounds impossible but trust me, it's true. Only another Averter will be able to tell what I am from sight. Well, not really sight. We have the ability to sense things that others overlook. For example, I always know when I'm being lied to. I can't tell what the exact lie is but I get a knot in my stomach every time I hear one; the bigger the lie, the tighter the knot. It's clearly not the most enjoyable ability for anyone to have but the older we get, the easier it becomes to tune the feelings out. You eventually get to a point where the only person's emotions you can tune into is the person you are assigned to. But I'll get to that later.

I live in a town called Sandes where my Dad works as a handyman and I go to school with all the normal kids. Dad's job is convenient because he is his own boss and we can leave town whenever we have to without raising too much suspicion. You can only stay in a town for four years, tailing the people you are assigned to, before you have to move on to another location. That way we don't get too attached to anyone and people also don't figure out what is happening to them. All Averters with young children have to live in small towns so that they can teach their children to master their abilities in a controlled environment. Imagine having to grow up in a city with millions of people throwing out millions of vibes all the time. Only adults who have mastered their craft could survive the surge.

The other tiny little thing is, according to my Dad, I am a bit of an anomaly as I am the only known female Averter that exists. I don't know why but our kind have always been men. Our lives are pretty much dictated from the start; a male baby is born from a union between a chosen woman and an Averter. The child is cared for by his mother for a year then handed over to the father, never to see his mother again. The father teaches him his responsibilities and at the age of twenty one, the son must carry on the tradition of our kind by creating a child with a chosen woman. That's our circle of life. Son begets son begets son, until there was me. Dad knew being a girl would make my future as an Averter different but as he wasn't sure how things would work out for me, he decided to bring me up exactly as his father brought him up. Study, study, study.

Once I had accepted all that I was meant to be, I realised that frivolous fancies and silly romantic notions were for the girls in my school and not for me. Why think about make-up and boys and all that nonsense when I knew that I had only four years to live in a town and that the clock to my age of motherhood was ticking? The way I saw it, if I couldn't have the life that they had, the freedom to choose what to do with my life, there was no point pining for it. It would have been as dumb as craving chocolate milkshake when you're allergic to cocoa. Plain stupid when my future was practically set in stone.

But then I had my first real jolt. Not the sensation I already mentioned that we feel when people are being dishonest. No, the jolts are much more than that. They are what you get when you sense that someone is going to do something really bad pretty soon. Like drink driving their father's car into the path of a truck, killing two passenger friends and ending a very promising tennis career. I had never felt anything so strong and so horrible before but that was what I sensed when I walked past Russ that Friday afternoon after our English lesson. Dad said that you know the people you are assigned to by the fact that you get these jolts from them. Everyone else is white noise, that person becomes real to you. Russ was my first.

Internally, I felt sick but somehow I barely flinched at the visual I had. Dad had prepared me well for that day. I was to let him know once I felt it and we would perform my first Aversion. Once I stopped Russ from going to the party, our bond would be sealed and I would be able to sense his irrational decisions without being in the same room as him. Most of Dad's people were his handyman job clients and so it was easy for him to avert them without anyone thinking that their meetings were out of the ordinary. Fortunately, we are not obliged to avert every single bad decision people make, only the ones that call out to us. If you're lucky, you only get to carry out an Aversion on someone once in your time with them.

That night, Dad and I waited on a bench across the street from Russ's family home. Dad was assigned to a couple of people on the same street so he knew exactly where to sit to not get noticed. Russ's parents were away on business trips and he had agreed to be the designated driver for his friends. It was some popular girl's house party and everyone was going to be there, even though it was a school night. Everyone but me, of course. At fifteen Russ was too young to be driving but that never stopped anyone in our town. Rules applied only to people who cared about the rules.

"Ready, Gem?" Dad said when the light in the hallway went out and the front door swung open.

"As I'll ever be," I replied, trying to sound confident about my task. I was so nervous that I could have been sick at any moment but I held my head up high and rose with Dad. I had been waiting for this moment all my life and I knew exactly what was expected of me.

At first Russ didn't notice us as he got into the car and prepared to reverse out of the driveway. Dad and I positioned ourselves in the path of his car and he finally spotted us. I saw him frown in his rear-view mirror reflection and I wondered what he was thinking at that moment. He probably had no clue who I was, even though we sat in a few classes together at school. I had perfected the art of remaining inconspicuous. No friends meant no questions about my alternative life. Easier than having to lie about it to people.

"It's all you, Gem," Dad smiled at me for a brief second then turned to wave at Russ who carried on looking at us in the mirror, probably curious as to why we weren't moving out of the way.

I took a deep breath and walked over to Russ's window, lowering my head to the same level as his face. Despite my common sense, I could see what half the girls in my year went on about when I overheard them going on about how cute he was. He had an appealing mix of his mother's Persian features and his father's athletic build. His dark eyes were wide and expressed his confusion, yet he said nothing. Funny how I had never noticed his eyes before; right then it felt like they were trying to bore holes through me. At least he was cautious enough not to wind down the window. But the glass only protected him physically. I didn't need to touch him for this to work. All I needed was eye contact and I had it.

Hello Russ. You will start to forget every word I say even as I speak. You will also forget that I was here tonight. There's no need to panic, going to the party is not an option. Do what you have to

4

do to get out of it. Whatever happens tonight, do not get into this car again.

That should do it, I thought as I saw his pupils dilate ever so slightly and flash a pale blue shade before clearing up again. But then I remembered something else that I had thought about earlier on that afternoon after I had felt the jolt and realised that I'd have to see him again that night.

Oh and stop that filthy habit of smoking with Dean and those idiots at break. Seriously, tennis pro with tar coated lungs?

I stepped away from the car and walked back to where Dad was waiting behind the car. It was time to see if it had worked, if I had finally crossed the threshold between exceptionally perceptive human and Averter. At first nothing happened as Russ remained in the car with his head bent low.

"I blew it, didn't I?" I said with a sigh.

"Patience. You've just attempted to alter his psyche, give it a moment."

Almost on cue, the car door flew open and Russ got out. He didn't turn back to acknowledge us. Instead he walked into the house and shut the door. Lights went on inside as he found his way round the house and Dad motioned for us to return to our waiting area. We had to make sure that he wasn't going to convince himself that the party was still a good place to be at. Dad said that sometimes it didn't matter what we tried to achieve, strong will power had been known to be the cause of failed Aversion attempts, especially when the subject was young and feisty. But the front door remained shut and after about an hour, Dad indicated that it was time to go.

That was it. My first Aversion. It was that easy. I was finally going to receive my Orb, a vessel that helped channel the emotions of our assignees to us from a great distance. Receiving it would truly mark my graduation into the big leagues.

I was certain things had gone smoothly until the next day at school when I walked past Russ in the cafeteria. I usually kept my head down when there were a lot of people around but I couldn't help sneaking a peek at him. I was still slightly fascinated by the fact that I had altered his mind and he was supposed to have no recollection of it. He was sitting with his usual group of noisy friends, probably the same ones who would have died last night if it hadn't been for my little stunt, so I expected him to be engrossed in whatever they were saying. But when I looked up, he was staring at me. Not just a quick glance like I was attempting, but outright staring. I was so shocked by this that I looked away really quickly. Something didn't feel right. I thought I had detected a flicker of recognition in his eyes. But it couldn't be. He had no reason to stare at me. It could only mean one thing.

I ate my lunch as hurriedly as I could, left the cafeteria and headed for the girls' toilets where I locked myself in a cubicle and tried not to hyperventilate. Maybe I was overreacting. Maybe he hadn't even been looking at me. I suppressed the urge to ring Dad and tell him that I might have botched the Aversion. What could I have done wrong? He hadn't gone to the party so that part had clearly worked. Maybe I hadn't been strong enough when I told him not to remember anything about me being there. That could be why he thought he recognised me.

I couldn't hide in there for long, I had classes to attend and our school toilets didn't smell good enough to hang about in for more than a few minutes. When I emerged from the cubicle, I caught sight of my reflection in the large mirror above the washbasins and gasped. I looked like someone had smacked me across the face and was coming back to finish the job off. I wasn't usually superficial enough to notice what I looked like so for me to say that I looked bad, I really did look awful.

"Gemma?"

I had left the toilets and was walking to my next class when the sound of my name hit me in the gut. Please let this not be happening, I prayed silently as I turned round to face my addresser.

Sure enough it was Russ standing behind me, frowning like he had done last night and still looking incredibly cute. I had never let myself consider what the boys in my school looked like and yet for the second time in less than twenty four hours, I was struck by Russ's large dark eyes. Urgh, what was wrong with me? Think cocoa allergy, I scolded myself.

Even worse than that was the thought that I had definitely messed up my first Aversion. I had to have. Russ Tanner had never spoken to me before today and suddenly, there he was, calling my name right in front of everyone. Damn it. That probably meant that I was not going to receive my Orb today.

TWO

"What?"

Rudeness had become my handy tool over the years. Who wanted to carry on conversation with a girl who couldn't be bothered to be civil? To my dismay, Russ smiled.

"Nothing. I figured you were heading to Lit class and since I'm going that way too..." He trailed off suggestively, his grin broadening slightly.

"You figured what? That you would walk with me?" I didn't wait for an answer before I turned and walked off. I hoped the smile had been erased from his face and I hoped even more that he wouldn't follow me. I had noticed a few people slowing down to hear what Russ Tanner had to say to the weird Gemma girl who never spoke to anyone. I hoped he was embarrassed enough by my action to back off. It must have worked because he came into our Lit class a few minutes after me and didn't look my way.

That was way too easy, I thought, but I was relieved when he didn't try to speak to me after the lesson. I should have known better.

"Why won't you talk to me?"

I jumped at the sound of his voice so close behind me. I

hadn't felt his presence at all, which was odd as I was supposed to be linked to him after what I had done to him the night before. I was on my way home after school, having no involvement in extracurricular activities meant I could leave the premises right after classes ended. Russ, on the other hand, usually joined in on whatever it was normal kids got up to and shouldn't have been following me. I recovered quickly and tried my most severe glare on him.

"What do you want from me? We've never spoken before today."

He stared at me for a few seconds as if trying to work out his answer, then he shrugged and smiled again. "I don't know. I guess I've wanted to say hello since the first day you arrived here but I never have. It's a bit silly really as we're in so many classes together. We clearly have things in common."

The annoying benefit of being an Averter was that I knew he wasn't lying. Even if I had somehow messed up his Aversion, he didn't seem to remember what I had done to him. It didn't feel like he was talking to me because he wanted to catch me out. I almost wished he had been untruthful. That would have been easier to understand; so much easier to deal with.

"No Russ, we don't have anything in common," I replied coldly, attempting impoliteness again.

"Ah, you know my name then?" He looked like he had just won the lottery.

"Everyone knows your name. We're supposed to cheer for you whenever you're on the court. I'm the one that should be asking how you know my name." I wondered if I could carry out an Aversion right then and make him stop bothering me. We weren't supposed to abuse our ability but surely if something had gone wrong from last night, no one would judge me too harshly.

He didn't get a chance to answer because someone yelled out his name from the school parking lot which was just a few meters away. It turned out he did have somewhere to be after all. A group of about five boys and girls were staring at him like he had gone insane and I wanted to yell back that I thought he had lost his mind too. One of the boys called his name again and Russ finally tore his gaze away from my face and turned to gesture to them that he was on his way.

"Look, I know you think us talking is a bit weird but it doesn't have to be. I would like to think we could be friends if we tried. This doesn't have to be like the movies where we don't speak because I'm an athlete and you're a…well, you're you."

"Russ!" His friends were getting more impatient. They were definitely going to interrogate him when he got back to them but he didn't seem to mind as he smiled at me and ignored them.

"See you tomorrow, Gemma Green."

I watched speechlessly as he turned and went to join his friends. That was by far the strangest thing that had ever happened to me and that was saying something if you considered the fact that I had been learning how to erase people's intentions since before I knew how to walk. How could I possibly have screwed up his Aversion that badly? How?

"You broke him."

Again I jumped at the sound of a male voice close behind me. How come all these people were creeping up on me today? When I saw the speaker, I relaxed a bit but I still wasn't happy. It was one of the four other Averters in our school. You didn't really think it was only little old me stationed at our school, did you? There are far too many problems in life for most schools to be left with only one trainee Averter.

The slightly overweight boy who had startled me was the oldest Averter of our lot and was two years ahead of me at school. There was another boy in his year and two other boys in the year below me. Although none of us ever spoke to each other, we could tell what we were. I knew by the fact that I couldn't read anything off them and also by the fact that when they first saw me, they had stared at me for much longer than I had stared at them. They were understandably shocked that I was a girl - their fathers must have had a lot of explaining to do when they got home – and it must have been difficult for them to accept that I wasn't just defective. By speaking to me, this boy had just made my day even weirder.

"What?"

"I said you broke him. You must have. He definitely remembers you."

"How do you…"

He hushed me by waving his hand in my face. "I've been doing this for three years and when I saw you today in the cafeteria, I knew you had finally carried out your first Aversion. A bit late if you ask me but I'm guessing that's not the first disappointment your father has had to deal with."

I was too shocked by his words to react. Dad had told me that some people were not pleased with the fact that he had decided to raise me as an Averter but I had never witnessed any hostility because of what I was.

The boy must have mistaken my silence for acceptance of his superiority because he carried on like he hadn't just been incredibly mean to me. "You must have done something you weren't supposed to. That's why he has a memory of you but not what you did to him. You're linked now and he knows it but he doesn't know why."

I should have been angry with him for being such an arse but what he said struck gold. Of course! Why didn't I think of that before? I had told Russ to quit smoking and that was not part of what I was supposed to change in his future. I was only meant to stop his party attendance and the resulting events and I couldn't even remember why I had added the smoking bit, but I had and here we were. I tried to calm myself down by thinking back to what Dad had taught me about failed Aversions but this was not quite a failed Aversion. I had carried out my task successfully, so what disaster did this fall under?

My next thought was that I had to tell Dad straightaway. He would know what to do. He might even have given me a scenario like this in the past as part of a test and I had forgotten.

"You're going to have to fix him on your own."

"What?" I must have sounded really dim to the boy. I hadn't formed a single complete sentence since he started speaking to me.

"If you tell your father, you set yourself back a few months at best. There was a boy who messed up an Aversion a few years ago." He paused and sucked in air through his teeth to convey the severity of the situation. "We've all been trying hard not to repeat his mistake."

Despite my annoyance at his smugness and my curiosity as to what the boy's crime and punishment had been, I had to swallow my pride and ask the question I felt was most important. As strange as it seemed, it sounded like he was trying to help me.

"And how do I fix him?" For obvious reasons, I didn't keep notes about what we did so I couldn't go home and search through my handy guide to being an Averter because there was none.

The boy shrugged and started to walk away. "Every one of them is different; it's impossible to tell what moves one in relation to another. You have to figure it out for yourself. Just hope it's something simple and quick."

"Wait!" I called out to him but he acted like he couldn't hear me and didn't turn around. My goodness, he was really going to leave me hanging.

I had to tell Dad. It was the only logical thing to do. He would be mad at me for making such a stupid error but at least he would have suggestions, or a hint as to what I could do next. I walked home at an incredibly slow pace as I tried to work out the best possible way to break the news to him without having my Orb confiscated. He had shown me my Orb last night when we got home and it had changed from its previous milky grey colour to a dark grey sphere. If I got my act together and carried out more successful Aversions, it would finally turn clear. Then I would be able to take it out of the house and use it the way it was intended.

But what if annoying greasy faced boy was right? What if Dad was so ashamed of my failure that he acted rashly? I couldn't imagine him punishing me too severely but I had never screwed anything up like that. If the boy could tell what had happened just by looking at Russ and I in school together, maybe others could too. Or maybe he was so incensed by the fact that I was allowed to be an Averter that he would go off and spread the word about me to others of our kind. I really had to tell Dad.

And I fully intended to until I got home and saw the banner he had put up in the kitchen. Yes, my Dad is soppy like that. It wasn't just the hand painted letters hanging above our kitchen table (it was obviously handmade because I'm pretty sure nobody stocks 'Hurrah, you're an Averter' banners in any store), it was the presence of a store bought lemon raspberry cake (my favourite) and a small wrapped box that swung it. I couldn't do that to him. I couldn't tell him I had failed, not when he had bought cake and a present. As I put on my biggest fake smile and returned his hug, I was immensely grateful that Averters do not have the ability to read each other's emotions (not for the first time in my life, I might add). He was too excited to notice anyway.

"It's for carrying your Orb when it clears up," Dad explained as I unwrapped the box and pulled out a soft velvet pouch. "My father didn't give me anything other than advice when he trained me but I wanted to make the memory of your first real day as an Averter a good one." He beamed at me. "I've always seen it as a second birthday, the day you finally wake up to what I've been going on about for years."

Even tough girls are allowed to tear up when their fathers do lovely things like that for them so I make no excuses for my watery eyes at that moment. But the tears were also there because I knew that I couldn't tell him about my little setback. It would break his heart. Imagine being saddled with a questionable product for the last fifteen years, only to find out it was definitely defective when put to the test. He didn't deserve that.

So I bit my tongue, ate my cake and went to school the next day with no plan as to how to fix Russ. I considered avoiding him for as long as I could but with us being in so many classes together, it was going to be impossible. Our first class together that day was third period so I spent most of the morning trying not to hyperventilate at the thought of a smiling Russ accosting me just before the lesson. I made sure I showed up as late as possible and avoided looking at anyone as I took a seat at the opposite end of the room to where he was sitting. Funny enough Russ said nothing to me that day. And he said nothing to me the next day either. Then it was the weekend (thank heavens) and on Monday, still nothing.

I began to let myself think that I was safe. Whatever it was I had done might have corrected itself. Maybe his brain had fought against the tweak and righted itself. By Tuesday I was sure of it and was even skipping along down corridors instead of cowering in corners to make sure Russ was nowhere in sight. Okay, maybe not skipping – I never skip – but I was returning to my old self. I began to let myself believe that the cautionary words of the annoying Averter were just his own paranoid projections. Oh, the wonderful joy of denial!

"Hi."

I was sitting in the library during my free period, trying to get a head start on a history assignment I had been given that morning. Let's not pretend I had anything more exciting to do with my time. I was a bit of a loner so if I wasn't sitting by myself in the library, I would have been sitting on my own somewhere else where no one would disturb me.

"Oh, it's you again," I sighed and rolled my eyes as I looked up and saw the young Master Tanner hovering over me with a grin on his face. He probably thought he was emanating coolness as he stood there with his arms across his chest and an air of nonchalance about him. Or maybe that was just me thinking that he looked cool. I tried to dispel the thought from my head.

"A few days late but as promised, I'm back." As he spoke, he pulled a chair towards the table where I was seated and settled down beside me.

I drew away instinctively. What did he think he was playing at? Leaving me hanging for nearly a week and then reappearing and acting like it was okay to promise to pester me and then not bother me at all. My goodness, why was I so mad at him for not stalking me over the last few days?

"I already told you I have nothing to say to you," I began to protest but he waved away my words like they were disturbing his ears.

"Seriously? You thought I'd give up that easily? I was only trying to give you some space. I reckoned I spooked you last week when I showed up out of nowhere and started talking to you but now, we've talked more than once so we're practically friends." He grinned again and I wanted to shove him off his chair to wipe the smile off his face. But I didn't.

I really wasn't sure how to play this. If he still felt the need to make a connection with me, he was probably still broken. I hadn't figured out if my best move was to try to fix him from a distance or let him think that I was being friendly then find out what it was I needed to do to get him back to normal. The second option sounded much quicker but then I would have to let him into my life, get to know him and all that nonsense. Not an appealing thought.

I was still trying to work out what my next words would be when something else happened that decided my course of action. I was not clumsy by nature. In fact I was pretty solid when it came to keeping myself in place, so I was surprised when I leaned forward on the table and knocked a pile of books to the floor. All my senses had been telling me to lean away from Russ but my body had reacted in a different way. The librarian looked over at us from her desk at the sound of the crash but she turned away when she saw it was me; I never caused any trouble so she must have understood that I'd had an accident.

But that's not what changed everything. After Russ and I had recovered from the initial shock of the projectile books, we both bent to pick up the offending objects. That was when our heads collided and that was when I felt my second jolt. This time I didn't have any flash-forwards, nothing at all came to my mind's eye. But I definitely felt a spark like I had done the week before and the weird thing was it looked like Russ had too. Yes, it made no sense that he could have but he stared at me in disbelief for a few long seconds, before shrugging off whatever thoughts were running through his head and picking up my books. He was clearly going to pretend that he hadn't felt whatever it was that had passed through me to him. Or was it him to me? I was so confused.

"This is not the best place to carry on a conversation," Russ laughed quietly and tried to continue in the same carefree tone he had spoken in before the jolt but I could tell that he was struggling. He was still thinking about what he had felt. Who could blame him? I was used to the idea of the supernatural and I was baffled as well.

It was strange but I felt something stirring in me. I desperately wanted to take away his confusion by carrying out an Aversion on him but I knew it would be wrong. The compassionate feelings I had were alien to me because I had never cared about anyone else in my life apart from Dad. There was no need to. Dad was all I needed, all I had till I turned twenty one. Everyone else was a distraction. I didn't care that the other Averters at school didn't carry on with the restricted life that I maintained; one of them was actually a very popular striker in the school's football team. But Dad had initially been overprotective about me because I was a girl and even though he had relaxed in recent years, it was difficult for me to pull down the walls he had built around me. So why was I finding myself drawn to Russ in such a strong way? I wondered if that second jolt had somehow ruined me even further.

"What?" Russ questioned me with a raised brow and I realised I had been staring at him.

"Nothing," I mumbled quickly then began to pack up my books as I tried to hide my embarrassment. "You're right; we should get out of here." As the words came out of my mouth, I knew I was committing myself to spending some time with him. And why not? Maybe annoying Averter boy had a point. Maybe the way to fix Russ was to spend a little time with him and see if I could find out how to make him forget whatever he remembered from that night.

As I thought of that night, something else came to me. "Do you smoke?" It might have sounded like a random question to him but it was worth a shot, right?

Russ actually grimaced. "Nicotine free since last week. It's a filthy habit and my body is a temple." He laughed at this and I was glad he was too occupied with his mirth to notice the expression on my face. He hadn't uttered the exact words I had said to him on that night but they were close enough. I scanned his face to see if there was any trace of recollection as to why he had stopped smoking but I couldn't read anything off him. He really believed he had stopped of his own accord.

"What?" Russ asked again.

I had to stop staring at him! He must have thought I was a total idiot or in-love with him or something and I certainly didn't want him to think any of those things.

"Nothing." I made sure not to look at him directly. "We really shouldn't be talking in here. If you want to talk, we can meet up later. Maybe after classes?"

As if on cue, the end of period bell rang and we both rose to head to our respective classrooms. I had French next and I was not looking forward to Mademoiselle Clarice (she insisted we call her this) making me stand at the front of class for five minutes for being late.

"That sounds great. We can go to The Hub…"

"Not The Hub," I interrupted. "Or Drums or Kicks or any of those places you guys like to hang out. If we're going to talk, doesn't it make sense to try somewhere half the school won't be staring at us?" I glanced around the corridor at the stream of students around us who were heading to their classes and I wondered if they were already thinking about the oddity of Russ and I talking in full view of everyone. I didn't usually care what people thought about me but that was because I wasn't dragging anyone down into the land of obscurity with me. I didn't want Russ to hate me next week when his senses returned and he discovered that he was now known as 'Gemma's friend'.

He frowned at me and shook his head. "I don't care about that but if it makes you feel more comfortable, where did you have in mind?"

"Pintos." It was a small café that I walked past on my way home and it was always either empty or full of older people and I knew we would be undisturbed there.

Russ seemed to know where I was talking about because he nodded, turned and disappeared amongst the crowd of kids heading away from me. And like that, it was settled. Russ Tanner and I were on the path to friendship.

THREE

Pintos was empty that afternoon. The usual two or three people that hugged its worn wooden tables, drinking lukewarm beers in the middle of the afternoon, were absent. I wasn't sure how the owner made any money from the establishment but I wasn't going to question their bad luck that day because it was the perfect venue for my chat with Russ. And yes, I was still naïve enough to hope that a simple conversation with him would unveil the reason for his defect. I hated keeping things from my Dad and I didn't want to drag my failure out any longer than necessary. Maybe if I asked Russ the right questions, he would be able to help resolve this issue quickly.

He came in a few minutes after I was seated and I saw him look around the café with distaste before spotting me in the corner and heading over with a smile.

"Great choice. No one in their right mind would want to eat in here so we're clearly safe," he joked and I tried not to smile.

He was right; I didn't want to order anything from the menu because the table reeked of what could only be stale vomit. Ingesting anything there would probably result in the production of said bodily discharge.

"Okay, I've never eaten in here but it seems perfect for conversation so let's talk. Isn't that what you wanted to do? Talk?"

Russ shrugged and picked up the menu to scan it. "And hang out, like two normal teenagers. Do you understand the concept?"

If only I could tell him that I really didn't understand the concept.

"See, that's my problem. I don't see why you want to hang out with me at all. You have all your friends. If you get fed up with them you can easily turn your attention to any other girl at school and they would have more to say to you than I ever would. Why do you want to talk to me? And why now?" I tried not to sound exasperated.

Russ put down the menu and stared intently at me. I felt slightly unnerved by the intensity of his gaze but I had to hold my own. I was good at this game, I had stared down scarier looking people on the bus. Strangely enough, Russ didn't waver. It was like he was trying to find something in my eyes, something to answer the unspoken questions he had, something to help him understand what the hell was going on.

Finally, he looked away and sighed. "Honestly? I don't know. I woke up one morning last week and you were on my mind. I had an uncontrollable urge to speak to you. Of course I'd always noticed you in class; you're kind of hard to miss, but I had never really felt that I could approach you. I always knew I would get shot down. But that morning, it felt like something was different. I knew that if I spoke to you, things would work out. And here we are, sitting in a dodgy little café, talking. I guess my instincts were right." He grinned and looked at me again.

My brain tried to process what he had just said. What did he mean when he said I was hard to miss? I thought I had perfected my blending in technique over the years. Apparently I still had some work to do. I was relieved to hear that all he had was a strange feeling and nothing more concrete but nothing else he had told me so far was helpful. I couldn't use any of it to fix him. I realised he was waiting for me to say something after a minute passed with us staring at each other in silence. Perhaps he wanted some reassurance that what he had said did not sound completely insane. Unfortunately, confirming his sanity would mean that I believed people could wake up and suddenly feel the need to speak to people they had never spoken to before.

"Is that what you tell all the girls?" I settled on counterattack, it was always safe to stay on familiar grounds.

At first Russ looked mortified at my question but he broke into slightly nervous laughter when he saw a smile tugging away at the corner of my lips. Why couldn't I have kept a straight face when I said that?

When he finally stopped laughing, he picked up the menu again and resumed playing with it. "I have always noticed you, Gemma. You probably don't remember the few times we spoke…"

"We've never spoken…" I began to protest but he cut me short.

"Last year on that field trip to see the War Memorial in Yates, you asked me to move over so you could get to your seat."

I stared at him in disbelief. "That doesn't count."

"Well, there was that time you couldn't reach a library book and I helped you get it. That was last year as well."

My mouth almost dropped open in shock. Those moments were barely memorable. I would never have counted them as mentionable in any conversation. It almost sounded like he…no, it wasn't impossible. Russ Tanner did not have a crush on me. This verbal diarrhoea had to be a result of whatever it was I did to him. I could sense that he thought he was telling the truth but surely he couldn't be. Why would he notice me? And I was not thinking that in an 'I'm-a-nobody-and-I-feel-sorry-for-myself' way. I was a social nobody but I knew I wasn't unattractive. I had caught boys looking at me even before I turned twelve and informed Dad that I needed a bra, so it couldn't just be my chest they were looking at. But I was nowhere near as pretty as some of the girls he hung out with. I didn't wear makeup like most of them did (lip balm did not count) but I allowed myself the little vanity of stud earrings and ensuring my hair was as healthy looking as it could be. Maybe Russ had a thing for pretty hair and silver studs.

"I wish you'd stop looking at me like that. Like I'm talking a load of nonsense," Russ's tone was convincingly hurt and I almost felt bad for him. But I had to remember what was happening here and try to gently steer him away from me.

"Look Russ, I know you think you want to be my friend but I assure you, this won't work. We don't have the same type of friends…what am I saying, I have no friends and we both know yours will not like me. If for some unimaginable reason I decide to hang out with you some other day, the only way we can talk in peace is by meeting up in places like this, where no one will know us. Do you really want that? What are you going to say to your friends when they ask where you've been? I don't know how else to convince you that us," I pointed at the both of us, "isn't practical."

"I don't want practical. I want you."

I don't think he intended to say those words out loud because he gasped at the same moment I did and then he turned an unnatural shade of red. This was way more serious than I had thought and I had no clue what to say in response to his unexpected confession. Whatever I had messed up had to be fixed fast.

We would have carried on staring at each other in embarrassed shock but, fortunately, we weren't allowed that luxury. The bored looking café owner, who had been waiting for us to indicate that we were ready to order, came over at that moment and waved her notepad at us.

"Cherry pie's our special today," she announced in a monotone voice as she eyed us and dared us not to order.

She had to be joking. The only thing I could have safely ordered in that place was a can of Coke, unopened.

My body rose before my brain acknowledged its movement. I had to get out of there before Russ said anything else that would make this situation worse – if it could get any worse.

"I have to…" I began to make my excuses.

"I didn't mean it to sound that way. You know what I meant, I just want us to be friends," Russ stood up as well and tried to salvage some of his dignity but that was the first lie I had read off him.

"So, no orders from you then?" The café owner glared at us as I practically ran out the door and Russ followed me. We probably wouldn't be allowed in there again.

"Gemma," Russ called after me. That was when I started to run. It felt stupid and childish running away from him, like I was not a trained Averter who could stare in the face of fate and alter it. What was wrong with me? Why was I acting like a silly little girl who had just been licked by one of the little boys in the playground?

Luckily Russ didn't chase after me. He probably felt that he would catch up with me again at school tomorrow. Urgh! I wondered if I could get Dad to call in sick for me but he would want to know why and I really, really didn't want to have to explain this to him. Running hadn't solved anything, just postponed the inevitable.

"Hey, Gem."

I was surprised to see Dad at home when I burst into the house. He told me he had a fully booked day unclogging pipes or doing whatever it was he'd been called out to do. But that was not what made me stop in my tracks. My father was a tall man with broad shoulders and a solid stance. Despite all his attempts to blend in, he was the kind of man that didn't go unnoticed in a crowd. Even when he was lying down, you could tell his carriage was poised. Today, hunched over the kitchen table, he looked like he was two feet shorter and had lost all the confidence he usually exuded.

"Dad, what's wrong?"

He tried to straighten up immediately he heard the concern in my voice but it was too late. I wasn't going to let him off and he knew it. Shaking his head slightly, he went over to the fridge and pulled out a can of Coke. Caffeinated drinks were as bad as it got with Dad when he was stressed out; he said alcohol messed up his abilities and he was too disciplined to ever allow that happen. "I had a little misunderstanding with someone. Nothing to worry yourself about."

There were many times I was grateful that we Averters couldn't tell each other's truths or lies but that day was not one of them. "Dad, I'm not a child anymore, I've had my first Aversion," I heard myself say in what I supposed was a reassuring voice. "You can tell me if there is something wrong."

He drained the contents of the can in one gulp before turning to face me again; this time I could tell he was struggling to stop from telling me the truth. Whatever happened to him had shaken him far beyond anything I had seen him go through and I was suddenly very afraid.

"Dad?" I didn't know what else to say.

He walked over to me and put his arms around me. He reeked of the powerful chemical he had been using at work earlier on but I didn't care. I hugged him back because I knew he needed the reassurance more than I did. He wasn't going to tell me what the problem was; he would have done so by now if he wanted to but something was preventing him from sharing his fears. I had a horrible feeling that whatever it was had to do with me and he was trying to protect me from the knowledge.

"All in good time, Gemma," he whispered softly and I felt myself nodding against his chest. I had trusted him all my life to make key decisions and so far he hadn't let me down. I had to believe that he knew what he was doing. "Tell me about your day."

Since my first Aversion, he had asked that I give him a quick summary of each day so that he could check if the process was going well. The idea was that he would stop keeping tabs on me when my Orb cleared up and I needed little or no guidance from him. Keeping the truth about Russ from him was one of the hardest things I had ever done and yet, for almost a week, I had managed to look him in the face and say nothing about my blunder. I felt awful. He might not be telling me the cause of his problems but at least I knew that he had problems. That had always been the nature of our relationship. Now I was turning into a horrible, horrible liar.

"Something happened today, actually," I pulled away from him, remembering the incident from the library. "I felt a jolt."

"That's good," Dad's voice picked up. "Was it someone new? Or the same boy? Remember what I told you; sometimes you get a few from the same person in a short period of time because whatever we've altered has affected another path which needs to be righted. It's usually small things but when you feel it…"

"No, Dad, it was really different," I had to interrupt him before he went into full lecture mode. "I…we touched and I felt something like last time but didn't see what I had to change. The weird thing is that I think he felt it too."

It was a good thing that Dad had stepped away from me when he started to give me the mini lecture because I could see the transformation on his face. He stared at me like he'd never seen me before, then he shook his head as if to clear the thoughts that were building up inside. A great sense of discomfort washed over me.

"I thought you said you weren't friends with that boy."

"We're not," I added hurriedly, "but we are in a few classes together and today we brushed past each other and I felt…something." The altered story rolled off my tongue with so much ease that I nearly gagged with disgust at myself. "Is that weird? That I would have seen nothing? And that it felt like he might have sensed something?"

Dad sank on to the high kitchen stool beside him and carried on looking at me. After what felt like an eternity, he answered. "No, it's not completely unusual. It's very rare that you would be able to pass on a jolt to someone but it has been done before. A very long time ago."

I could tell he was drifting away with his memories and I waited for him to expand on what he had just said but after a minute or so of silence, I realised he was done talking. My question, coupled with whatever had happened to him earlier on in the day, was proving too much for him to cope with. Seeing this side to my father freaked me out but I knew it wasn't the right time to press on so I picked up my school bag and left him with his thoughts.

The first thing I noticed when I got to my room was that my Orb, which Dad had finally given me the night before and which I had carefully placed on my pillow before I left for school, was no longer a dark grey colour. No, it was much worse than that. It had turned a florescent shade of orange.

FOUR

I had my third jolt the next day. I was so preoccupied with trying to avoid Russ that morning at school that when the jolt came, I was completely unprepared for it. The girl's name was Emily Shores. I didn't know her because she was only thirteen and I had never noticed her before. Our school wasn't big but we weren't so small that everyone knew everyone. At first I wasn't sure that the vision I saw was right. What flashed before my eyes, as I sat in my Art class listening to Mrs Jones rattle on about Baroque painters, shocked me more than what I had seen happen to Russ.

The girl was in an isolated place with a boy who looked much too old for her to be hanging out with. He was a boy I recognised from the year above mine. Lanky and a little bit awkward, he played drums in a band that always shoved their gig flyers in my face when I walked through the cafeteria. I didn't dislike him but what I saw made me so mad that I wanted to walk right up to him then and punch him in the face. I had no idea why she was out in the middle of nowhere with him but he had no right to try on anything with her. She had been flirting with him but she was a kid, he should have known better. The good part of my vision was that nothing came of his aggressive advances on her; she managed to break free and run to safety. But Emily Shores would be so scarred by the event that some prospects of her future self would be destroyed.

It wasn't that bad things weren't going to happen to her in her lifetime, she would never learn any lessons in life otherwise; it was just that her future self was calling for this Aversion to happen. Just like Russ's future self and the lives of his friends had thrust my first Aversion on me. Don't ask me why it works this way; I don't make up the rules about Fate and Destiny, I just play my part.

The worst thing was that I knew that the event was going to happen later that afternoon. I would have to carry out the Aversion before she left school because she was planning to leave the building with him. I wished I had my Orb sorted out. That way I would have been able to attempt an Aversion from a distance. But with everything as muddled up as it was, I was going to have to corner Emily fast. The only place I could think of was the girls' toilet at lunchtime but that meant I would have to lurk outside till she showed up. What if Emily didn't have to use the facilities? Would I miss my classes waiting there for her to turn up? And what about the dozen or so other girls who were sure to be in there?

"Hey."

For an Averter I was pretty useless at detecting when Russ snuck up on me but I could be forgiven that day. I had given up lunch to stalk Emily, only to discover that she was stuck like glue to another girl in her year. They had spent most of their lunch break picking at their food as they ogled boys in the cafeteria and giggling whenever anyone looked their way. It was pretty pathetic to watch but I had to endure it as I had to find my chance to speak with Emily. It looked like my biggest problem would be getting her away from her friend so when Russ spoke to me, I was a little bit agitated and not in the mood to tackle his obsession with me.

That was what I thought when I heard his voice, but certainly not what I felt when I spun round and looked into those huge eyes of his. He was standing much too close to me; he was tall but I had taken my height from my father and I stood almost level with him. Our faces were inches away from each other and I noticed his lips curl up in appreciation as he scanned my face up-close. I wanted to step back but my legs weren't listening to my brain. For some reason, I blushed as I recalled his regrettable words from yesterday. *I don't want practical. I want you.*

"Hey," he said again as he took the initiative to step back. He must have noticed my discomfort and didn't want to scare me off like he had done last time. He took another step back and ran his fingers through his hair as he smiled sheepishly at me.

His smile is not cute.

His smile is not cute.

His smile is not cute.

I repeated the words silently, knowing that I was only kidding myself. His smile was cute and I had noticed that I really, really liked the way his eyes settled on me and me alone. I hated myself for being such a typical girl. This was no way for someone in my line of existence to feel. I couldn't let the first boy that thought he liked me throw me off my life's mission. Get a grip Gemma!

I was ready to dive into another lecture about why he should leave me alone when an idea came to me. It was a little bit funny that the attention he was giving me was the reason I had the idea in the first place.

"I need your help."

I think my request threw him off completely because he tilted his head back and frowned, then looked around like I might have been speaking to someone else.

"I need you to extract that girl over there from the other one wearing the green headband. Only for a couple of minutes, please."

"Why?" Russ asked reasonably.

"If you do this, I will devote my entire afternoon after school to you." I didn't know what made me say it but the words came tumbling out before I could stop them.

He smiled like I had just handed him a golden ticket. "I have tennis practice till five…"

"That's fine; I'll meet you after practice." Better for me, I thought, hoping I would only spend an hour with him in the end.

"I have a better idea, you can sit on the bleachers and watch me play so I won't have to look for you afterwards."

It was almost like he didn't believe I'd show up to meet him at five. I guess he had no reason to trust me, not after I ran away from him once. What was I supposed to do for a few hours on the bleachers? Sit in the hot sun and watch him play a boring game? I wanted to argue but time was running out.

"Deal. Now go do your bit."

It took seconds for him to fulfil his part as the overly excited girls gasped in disbelief at the fact that Russ Tanner was speaking to them. Emily's friend looked like she was about to wet herself when Russ gently pulled her away. Even from that distance, I caught a glint of jealousy in Emily's eyes and I almost felt bad about what I was doing to their friendship but there were more important things to tackle.

I put on an air of indifference as I walked over to the table where Emily sat and I slid on to the seat her friend had just vacated. The cafeteria was crowded but, fortunately, the table the girls had chosen to stare at boys from was a little out of the way so we were the only ones occupying it. Before Emily had the chance to acknowledge the fact that someone was sitting so close to her, I held her gaze.

Emily, you will start to forget every word I say even as I speak. You will also forget that I was sitting here beside you today. There is no need to panic. You cannot hang out with Gerry Pane today no matter how badly you want to. Do what you have to do to get out of it.

Although I also wanted to discourage her from hanging out with Gerry in future, I made sure not to say anything else to her. After what had happened with Russ, I had to be careful. What if I meddled again, broke her too and had to deal with two confused strangers following me around school. I wasn't even sure if what I had done would work for her, seeing as I was defective, but it was safer to keep things to the book and see what happened.

I left the table and went back to where I had been standing before, hoping that my actions had gone unnoticed. I didn't think people usually paid much attention to what I did anyway. Russ was still chatting to the other girl and Emily had resumed glaring at them; it was almost as if I hadn't entered the picture at all. When Russ glanced my way, I nodded and he said something to the girl to end their conversation then started to walk towards me. That wasn't what I had intended by my nod. I had only wanted him to know that he could go. I didn't want to spend the last ten minutes of my lunch break with him, especially if I was going to be trapped with him for the entire afternoon after school.

"You're not going to tell me what that was about, are you?" he asked once he got close enough to whisper to me.

"Nope," I flashed him a false smile and tried to focus on my long overdue lunch. As I unwrapped the ham and cheese sandwich I had prepared that morning, I wondered if he noticed that I hadn't spoken to Emily at all when I sat beside her. Or if he wondered why my contact with her had been so brief. Why go through all that trouble of getting him to distract her friend if all I wanted to do was sit by her for ten seconds?

Russ stared at me like he wanted to push the issue a little more but he decided against it and sighed. "Okay, just as long as you haven't involved me in a drug deal or anything like that. I can't afford to get kicked off the tennis team."

"I would never..." I began to protest my innocence at such a preposterous suggestion but he laughed and turned away before I could finish my sentence.

"See you after school," he called out as he went to join his friends at the other end of the cafeteria. I allowed myself a peek their way and saw that they didn't bother questioning him this time about why he had been talking to me or to Emily's friend for that matter. Maybe he had concocted a story for them after the last time they had seen us together or they simply didn't care that he was fraternizing with me. Either way, it didn't matter. I had carried out my second Aversion and I had him to thank for it.

It was only then that I realised that I had done something that would be considered really, really stupid by any other Averter. I had asked one of the people I was supposed to be looking out for to help me carry out an Aversion. Granted, he'd done so unwittingly but there had to be something wrong with the fact that I solicited his assistance. Goodness, what was wrong with me? I had ruined my first Aversion by being meddlesome and now I had possibly set the undoing of my second one in motion.

Paranoia crept over me as I glanced around the cafeteria, searching for signs of any of the others. Surely if they had seen what I had done, their disapproval would show on their faces. But no one was paying any attention to me. The boy who had pointed out my initial error with Russ was sitting with another boy at the other end of the large room and they appeared to be engrossed in conversation. I was relieved that I couldn't locate any of the other Averters in the room but I almost wanted someone to have noticed so that I could gauge how bad the situation was from their reaction. Only time would tell if I had messed this one up too.

When I went back to classes after lunch, I tried to push the thought of my promise to Russ out of my head. What had I been thinking? A whole afternoon trapped in his company? Watching him play tennis would probably be the easy part, I could do my homework during that time, but the hours after that scared me. I was pretty new to the whole "friendship" business and things would be even more uncomfortable now that I suspected that he actually liked me. The only reason I had offered to spend time with him was because I knew he would jump at the idea and I needed to sort out the Emily issue.

Thinking of Emily helped pull me back to the real problem at hand. To ensure I had carried out her Aversion correctly, I planned to follow her after school and make sure she didn't leave with the drummer. I wouldn't be able to follow her all afternoon (that would be sheer madness) but it would make me feel better to see what she intended to do with the rest of her day. Russ would understand if I arrived at his practice a little bit late.

By three thirty I was waiting outside the school building, watching as the other students trooped out to freedom. In my vision, Emily had been with the drummer in daylight so I figured that if she didn't meet him before six o'clock when the sun began to set, all would be well. We were not usually supposed to stalk the people we helped but I had to be certain that it had worked.

Emily came out of the building with her headband friend from the cafeteria and another girl. They were chattering away as they headed towards Hound Street where all the shops were. Perhaps that was a good sign; if they got carried away window shopping, my vision would not come true. I was going to follow them all the way down the road and for as long as I could, just to be sure, but I stopped when I saw the drummer emerge from the building and head straight for the group. I felt the blood drain from my face and rush to my heart which was beating at an unimaginable rate.

Emily was clearly friends with the drummer because none of her friends flinched when he came up to them and started to speak to her. I was too far away to decipher what they were saying but their actions were enough for me. He appeared to request something of her and she looked at her watch then shook her head. What did that mean? That she wasn't going to go with him? Or that she wasn't free to go with him yet? I felt a bead of sweat forming on my brow and I exhaled the breath I had inhaled ever since he walked into the scene. He said something else to her and now she looked annoyed as she responded with another shake of her head. Then, just like that, my prayers were answered as he stormed off in a huff at whatever it was she had said to him. Emily looked a little upset but one of her friends said something to her and she shrugged before they carried on towards the shops.

It had worked! Maybe I wasn't broken after all. And even if I was, I had still managed to carry out this Aversion successfully. I tried not to think of the possibility of Emily remembering me tomorrow, just as Russ had. I would cross that bridge if I came to it. That was my job done for Miss Shores, at least for now. If she decided to meet up with the drummer tomorrow and he tried anything on, I had no say in the matter. That would be the day she was supposed to learn whatever lesson it was that life had in store for her. I couldn't follow her around fixing everything in her life.

I suddenly realised that I didn't like this whole Aversion business as much as I had convinced myself I should. I had thought all along that it was my duty to help people by ensuring that their fate remained on the right track but I had never considered how difficult it might be to watch the rest of their lives play out and not be able to do anything to fix all the bad. Despite my successful mission, I walked over to the school's tennis court with my shoulders hunched and a frown on my face.

Getting there, I was surprised to note that I wasn't the only spectator present for the practice session. A group of younger girls stood pretty close to the court, shrieking with delight whenever Russ and his practice partner's shirts rose higher than their navels. I couldn't help smiling at this sight. I know I said all that about avoiding chocolate milkshake if you are allergic to cocoa but let's be honest, I wasn't exactly allergic to cocoa. I was just on a strict diet that prohibited its consumption. Inhaling the aroma of a warm mug of cocoa certainly wouldn't harm me, would it? I almost didn't blame the girls for being so childish; even I had to admit that their abs were impressively cut. It didn't help that both boys were also easy on the eyes. But I was surprised that the coach didn't try to get rid of their adoring fans; he probably thought that the distraction served as crowd simulation of a real tournament.

I tried to ignore them and focus on the homework I had brought with me but the players grunted so loudly with every shot of the ball that I couldn't concentrate. I gave up after a few minutes and watched the boys run around the court instead. Russ was completely engrossed in the game so I didn't think he noticed I was there at all. If I had known I wouldn't be missed, I would have stuck with Emily to make sure she was really okay. I gritted my teeth and tried to enjoy the session but I had never been keen on sports and had no clue what was really happening.

By the time the coach called an end to the practice, it was past five and the younger girls had lost interest and moved on to harass some other boys. Russ finally looked up at the bleachers and saw me. I wished he didn't look so happy as he made his way towards me.

"You weren't here when we started; I thought you'd bailed on me." He grinned as he sat on the bench below me. His T-shirt was stuck to his chest with sweat from all that running around. I hated the fact that my gut reacted to his presence beside me. Why couldn't he be grotesque looking and horrible to me? Why couldn't he tell that I didn't want to be there with him?

"I said I'd be here," I rolled my eyes and stood up. "I have to be home by seven so if you want to do anything other than sit here, I think we'd better get going."

Russ looked a little shocked by my abruptness, probably because he thought we had bonded a little bit at lunchtime, but I intended to maintain some control of our afternoon together. I hadn't forgotten what had happened yesterday.

"Oh okay," he muttered then took a whiff of his shirt and

wrinkled his nose. "I'm going to confess, I didn't really think this through. I need to take a shower but if I use the school's changing room, we won't have much time left to spend together. Plus, I'm starving and I don't have enough cash on me to stop off for food…"

Thank God, he was going to cancel! My heart leapt with joy at the thought but it quickly fell as he carried on.

"…so I was wondering if you would mind stopping over at my house for a bite to eat instead. My mum's at home so I promise you'll be perfectly safe waiting with her as I get changed. She makes really good sandwiches too."

Was he really asking me to go to his house and meet his mother? What teenage boy in his right mind did that? Unless they really had no ulterior motives. Or perhaps he was lying about his mother being at home. But I didn't read any vibes off him so I knew that couldn't be it. That was one of the many moments I wished I was a mind reader as well as an Averter.

I wanted to insist that he should shower at school and offer to buy him a sandwich but something in the way he looked at me stopped me. I could sense the intensity of his need for me to say yes and when I found myself shrugging and nodding, it didn't feel like the wrong thing to do. Besides, if he tried anything funny, I could try to block his thoughts to protect myself. I reckoned I would be forgiven if I had to break a rule or two in my lifetime.

"Great!" he exclaimed with relief and grabbed the sports bag he had set down on the bench. "I don't usually ask any girl to come home with me…"

"But you feel a special connection with me so it's fine, right?" I muttered this to myself but Russ stopped and fixed me with a glare that sent shudders down my spine.

"You don't get it, do you? You think this is my idea of a joke. I wish I could show you how this feels." He looked really angry for the first time since he had started following me and I wondered if it would be wiser to leave him and head home. But he had helped me out and I had promised him my time. Dad had taught me never to go back on a promise and I wasn't going to start breaking that rule because Russ Tanner was throwing a hissy fit.

"Fine, fine, don't bite my head off. I'll stop joking about it. I'm just not used to this kind of attention. I'm still trying to work out your angle." I admitted to him.

"And I'm still trying to work out why the hell I can't stop thinking about you," he countered exasperatedly and that shut me up, just like his revelation yesterday had. I felt bad that I knew why he was suddenly obsessed with me but I couldn't relieve his frustration without sounding like a lunatic to him. Not that I was considering telling him the truth.

As we walked on in silence, we received puzzled stares from a few students who were still hanging around the school building. It was Russ's reputation that was on the line for being associated with me and if he didn't care, who was I to worry? The only comfort I got out of our twenty minutes walk to his house was spotting Emily and her friends sitting outside a café when we went down Hound Street. But even that didn't stop me from remaining a little annoyed with Russ. If he was so annoyed with me, why didn't he just let me go home?

"Sorry I snapped at you," Russ's apology came out of nowhere as we approached his family home on DuPont Street. I had been trying really hard to look like I had no clue what house his was but he had other things on his mind. He probably wanted to make up with me before we got to his house. Perhaps he knew his mother would sense that I was not a willing participant in this venture and he wanted to make sure I was appeased.

I considered letting him suffer for a little longer but I gave in when I saw how upset he looked. "It's okay. I shouldn't have provoked you either."

"It's just...I can't explain what's happening and I..." He stopped suddenly when we got to the driveway outside his home. "Yesterday, at the library, did you feel anything when we..."

Oh no, he was bringing it up! I had hoped he had suppressed all thoughts of the jolt. In fact, a foolish part of me had been hoping I had imagined it all. But it must have happened because it was clearly one of the things bothering him. I glanced nervously at the two storey detached brick house he called home and then back at him as I tried to think of a crafty response but my silence was the answer he needed.

"You felt it too, didn't you?" His eyes widened. "I could have sworn I saw something as well but I must have imagined that part. If you felt something too then maybe I'm not going insane." The relief in his voice was heartbreaking.

That was when I started to really worry. Ever since I found out that Russ had a recollection of me, I thought I had been operating on a level of fear but it turned out I was in for a surprise. The ball of dread that settled in my gut was now so heavy that I felt like heaving. I felt trapped by the gravity of my guilt at causing him so much pain. This was not how things were meant to pan out. What had I been thinking? I should never have come back to the scene of the crime with him. I should have told Dad right from the start and not put myself in this avoidable awkward position.

Russ saw the panic flicker in my eyes and he knew I was about to make a run for it. Even though I could tell he had sussed my intention, I tried to flee anyway. But he wasn't planning to let me get away so easily this time. I had barely taken a step back when he reached out and grabbed my hand, pulling me close to him. I had not been prepared for my first three jolts and I was certainly not prepared for the one I felt when Russ's hand made contact with mine. The scene I saw was a flashback to the moment when I stopped him from driving off to the party the other night, but that was not what drained the blood from my face. No, what did it was the disbelief on Russ's face as he held on tight to me and had the bad fortune to share in my vision.

FIVE

Flight was now completely out of the question but I had no idea what I was supposed to do. I wondered if this was the right time to use the emergency mind fritz trick Dad had taught me but my conscience wouldn't let me brainwash Russ to protect myself. I had screwed with his mind enough already. After his warped Aversion, whatever it was I had unknowingly done to him at the library and now, who knew what I would achieve if I tried messing with his mind again? Something was clearly wrong with my abilities and for some reason Russ was the one bearing the brunt of it. I had to figure out why things were going so wrong but at the moment I had a confused teenage boy to deal with. One who was gripping my arm too tightly.

"Russ, you're hurting me," I kept my voice low and my tone even. He didn't need to know that I was as terrified as he was. Maybe if I maintained some composure and didn't confirm what he had just seen, he would think his mind was playing tricks on him.

He let go of my arm but he was standing so close to me that I knew he wouldn't hesitate to grab me again if I tried to take a step back. His eyes were round with the shock of what he had seen, yet clouded with doubt at the authenticity of it all. "You were here last week, I saw you. You did something to me that night. That's why I keep thinking about you. Did you drug me?"

I let him speak because it gave me time to think about what my next line of action would be. Dad had not prepared me for this eventuality so I was going to have to wing it for now and pray that he had a solution to this fiasco.

"Russ, maybe we should go inside. You're exhausted and I think a shower and a meal will help."

"No, no," he insisted, "don't try to pretend this is nothing. I touched you and I felt something, I saw something. It was right here, you came out of nowhere and told me not to go to that party and I listened to you. I don't know why, but I did. It was like my life depended on it."

If only he knew.

"And then you asked me to stop smoking and then you were gone. How come I didn't remember any of that until now? Stop looking at me like that; I know I'm not crazy. You were here. Just say you were here."

"Russ…"

"Say it!" He yelled at me this time and I took a step back, not because I thought he would hit me but because his mother had appeared at one of the windows and was frowning at us.

"I'll see you in school tomorrow when you've calmed down." I took another step back, counting on the fact that he wouldn't reach for me again now that his mother was watching us. He watched in silence as I took a few more steps away from him before I turned and ran. Maybe he didn't try to stop me because I had stunned him with visions he couldn't understand the last two times he had tried touching me. His reasoning didn't matter to me at that moment, I was just glad that he hadn't decided to follow.

I was out of breath by the time I got home and collapsed onto my bed. Tears had started to flow once I got to the comfort of my street and it felt good. I had been choking back a lot of emotions over the last few days and I hadn't realised the amount of anxiety that had been building up in me. It wasn't easy to accept that I was defective. Being the only female Averter around was bad enough but then not being good at what I was born to do? The thought was killing me. Maybe I wasn't cut out for this after all. Maybe Dad had wasted all those years training me for nothing. He had come across doubters over the years and now all he had to show for his resilience was a dud child. I sobbed into my pillow as I tortured myself with those thoughts. This was unusual behaviour for a girl who hardly ever cried but I was accepting that things were rapidly changing in my life. I might as well stop trying to pretend to be one of the boys and accept my fate.

Dad was still out but I knew once he came home I would tell him the truth. I would tell him all of it. There was no point acting like this was just a tiny flaw anymore. I had put our identities in danger by letting Russ share in that vision and something had to be done about it. Why had I listened to that boy at school and tried to sort this out on my own? I remembered the contempt in his voice as he spoke to me and wondered if this had been his intention all along. Get me to keep the facts from Dad and then screw things up so much that they would make an example out of me.

I must have cried for a good half hour before I heard movement in the house. My face was swollen and blotchy and my hair was stuck to the side of my face but I didn't care. A part of me hoped that if Dad saw me looking so remorseful and wretched, he would be less inclined to yell. Not that Dad ever yelled. He was the only genuinely gentle soul I knew. But I had never given him cause to be enraged. This would surely be a test of the depth of the love he had for me.

"Gem," I heard him call from downstairs when he realised I was home. I wondered if I should let him enjoy a few more minutes of normalcy before I landed the blow on him but who knew what damage Russ's knowledge of my abilities was doing already?

Facing Dad in the kitchen was officially the hardest thing I had ever done in my life. The alarm on his face when he registered my appearance was agonizing. I decided not to give him a chance to speculate. That would be much worse than the truth.

"I'm so sorry Dad, I should have come to you all along." I blurted out the whole story, right from what I had added to Russ's Aversion to what had happened about an hour ago. The words that left my lips were heavy but strangely therapeutic. By the time I was done speaking, I had settled down on one of the kitchen stools and Dad had turned a sickly pale shade. But he hadn't interrupted me or started yelling. I couldn't tell if that was good or bad.

I waited for the outburst but nothing came. Nothing at all. Instead he stared off into the distance, as if contemplating his next move. Or maybe he was just recovering from the shock of what he had just heard. I knew not to push him; when my punishment came, I would bear it with honour. I would do whatever he asked of me if he knew how to resolve this mess.

"Start gathering your things Gemma, we need to leave this place."

"What?"

I'm not sure what I had been expecting but it wasn't that. Were my actions so bad that this was the only solution? Running away?

"It should take me a couple of weeks to get us relocated so you don't have to rush too much." It was as if he hadn't heard me speak.

"Wait Dad, is that it? We run? We still have a few months left before our four years here are up. What about all the people we are supposed to help? What about Russ? He must think he's lost his mind..."

"This is the only way," Dad snapped at me and I had to admit I was a little relieved at his reaction. It felt like what he should have been doing right from the start.

I threw my hands up and shook my head in bewilderment as I got back on my feet. "But why? Why can't we fix this? We can ask for help if we don't know what to do. That boy from school..."

"You will not ask anyone else for help, you hear me?"

This time I was frightened by the rage in his voice. We never discussed other Averters in the past and I had always assumed it was because we never had any use for them. Dad's irritation by my words made it feel like there was more to it than that. He must have realised that he sounded very far removed from himself because he took a deep breath and then carried on in a calm voice.

"Maybe I should explain. This thing that has happened between you and the boy is unusual but it is not the first time I've heard about it. The good news is it is not your fault. Well, not completely. The bad news is, now that he knows what has happened, you can't take away his memories of it. We don't carry out Aversions to aid ourselves when things don't work out quite as they should have." He paused and sighed. "The best solution is for us to remove ourselves from here as quickly as we can without raising further suspicion. I wish I could tell you that I knew of a way to reverse what has happened but I don't."

I felt that he was keeping something from me but I couldn't tell what. Why would he not disclose a solution to me if he knew of one? Hopefully whatever it was that I was detecting didn't matter. I trusted Dad and if he said that this was the only way out of the problem, I had to believe him. But I still had to ask one question that had been on my mind.

"So...it's not because I'm a girl? That's not why this is happening?" As I voiced my fear of innate failure, I realised that this was the one thing I was most anxious about. Messing up was one thing, messing up without having any control over it was another. If all this madness was because of something else other than who I was, then maybe I could still make Dad proud in the future.

For the first time since my confession, I saw Dad's expression melt into what looked like sympathy. Then he finally did what I had hoped he would do all along as he crossed the little distance that was between us and hugged me. Words have never been able to describe the sense of security and comfort Dad's hugs gave me. I started to feel a little bit better about the prospects of our conversation.

"No Gem, it's not because you're a girl. You're special in many ways but being different from the rest of us is a good thing. Don't ever let anyone make you feel like you're not good enough. We have to protect ourselves though so whatever happens, you can't speak to that boy again. He will have questions for you but if you avoid him, he won't be able to confirm anything."

I didn't like the sound of that. Ignoring Russ wasn't going to solve anything if I had to see him every day at school for the next two weeks. I already knew how persistent he was. Now he would be even more insistent on stalking me. "So we ignore everyone and then we run away. Don't you think we need some more time to think this through? What about school? How do I avoid Russ there?"

"That shouldn't be a problem as you are not going back. I'll homeschool you. It will only be for a short time so you won't be missing out on too much."

I had no idea where it came from but as his words registered, I suddenly felt a foolish bond of loyalty towards my school and all its members. Despite the fact that I had never really cared for the institution, I couldn't bear the thought of never going back there. Leaving on short notice was bad enough but it was doable. However, the thought of never walking down those crowded halls again, of never hearing Mrs Jones's voice as she destroyed all hopes of me liking the Rococo Era, of never cowering over my sandwich in the cafeteria to avoid attention, of never seeing that annoying grin on Russ's face again - I didn't think I could manage it.

That last thought especially took me by surprise. I knew

Dad was right and I was supposed to avoid Russ from now on but all the senses in my body were piqued at the thought of leaving him hanging in a state of limbo. Or maybe that wasn't it. Maybe I had become so used to trying to avoid him over the last few days that it was taking a little while to acknowledge the fact that I would never see him again. Ever. It wasn't a completely irrational thought; he was the only one I had said more than ten words to since I got there. As crazy as it sounded, he was the closest thing I had to a friend. Russ and I, friends. It was almost laughable.

"You said this is not the first time this has happened. What went wrong the last time?"

Dad had not expected me to ask that because his eyes narrowed before he looked away and went to the fridge to pull out ingredients for preparing dinner. I knew I wouldn't like what he was going to say next.

"Death and pain, that's what happened. I don't want that for you, or for anyone else for that matter. Trust me Gem, this is the only way."

But it couldn't be. Why didn't I believe him?

"What if I promise not to speak to him," I blurted out, knowing that this was a lie. "You know I can do it. I've spent the last few years staying clear of everyone and I really don't want to..."

Dad laughed nervously as he started to chop up some vegetables. I couldn't understand how he even remembered that we needed to eat dinner. "Do you think I'll be that bad a teacher? You can't stomach a few weeks with me to keep you safe? You'd rather go and face that boy again?"

"Running doesn't solve anything. I'm pretty sure Russ will find out where we live and he'll be at our door everyday till I come out and face him. Hiding will make it more obvious that I have something to conceal from him. At least if I show up at school and act like he imagined it all, he might accept that." I didn't believe the words as I said them. There was no way I could fool Russ into accepting that he had imagined what he saw, not after I had seen the look on his face outside his house. My acting skills weren't that good, but did Dad know that?

I wasn't sure why I was fighting so hard to go back into the lion's den but it felt like it was the thing to do. Not necessarily the right thing to do, just what I was meant to do. Dad must have had an idea of what was going on in my head because he stopped chopping the head of lettuce he had been holding and fixed me with a cold stare.

"You would go back and face him despite all I've said?"

The problem was that he hadn't really said anything to convince me that staying home was a good move. All he had said was that we were leaving because I couldn't wipe Russ's slate clean. And that it wasn't really my fault that he had remembered. If we were in such grave danger, why weren't we leaving the next day as opposed to in two weeks?

"What's really going on Dad?" I asked in what I hoped was a soft tone.

But answering that direct question must have been more than he could handle. He stared at me for a little bit longer before speaking. "Bring me your Orb."

Of course, my Orb! I hadn't checked it since it had turned orange yesterday. I wasn't sure if I wanted to show Dad yet another sign of my failure but I had no choice. He clearly felt it had a say in the decision he was about to make. Or perhaps he intended to confiscate it. I only hesitated a little before I went upstairs to retrieve it from the drawer where I had hidden it. I didn't bother taking it out of the velvet pouch as I handed it to Dad. Maybe the shock would be lessened if it looked like I had no idea it was the wrong colour.

"Fine, we'll try your way. You go to school tomorrow and if he doesn't hound you down by the end of the day, you can carry on going till we leave. But if there is any hint of trouble, you have to tell me Gemma. No more secrets."

It wasn't Dad's sudden turn around that caused my mouth to drop open. His words paled in comparison to what he was holding in his hand. The Orb he had pulled out of the pouch, the same one which had shone an embarrassingly bright fluorescent orange yesterday, was now clear as crystal.

SIX

That night, I found it impossible to fall asleep. I couldn't understand why the miraculously cleared up Orb was enough to convince Dad that it was okay for me to go back to school. He had suggested that one of the possible reasons things had gone wrong was because my system was still trying to adjust to the new connections I was making. Now that the Orb was in its proper state of operation, I wouldn't need to make so much of an effort to carry out Aversions. The jolts I received would be cushioned by the energy the sphere emitted and I could work my magic from a distance.

This didn't explain why the Orb had turned orange or why it had cleared up so quickly. Orbs are handed down from generation to generation and mine had belonged to my great-grandfather so there was a chance that it had been defective when he died but no one else had known. Seeing as the only way to find out was by admitting to Dad that it hadn't always been grey, I figured it wouldn't hurt to let the issue slide.

But that wasn't what kept me up. For hours, all I could recall was Russ's expression when he realised that I had done something to him, that his obsession with me was not without reason. Even though he had been unable to make sense of what he had seen, he had looked slightly relieved. It was almost like it was more important to him that he wasn't losing his mind. I wondered how he would react when I showed up at school the next morning. I also wondered why it had bothered me so much that I might never see him again and why I was now the one struggling to get him out of my mind.

When I finally drifted off to sleep, my dreams were filled with images of Russ too. In all of them, he chased me down the eerily empty hallways at school and caught me just as I broke into the abandoned cafeteria. When he grabbed me, the jolts we felt were more powerful that anything I had experience in real life, almost explosive. And each time I woke up with a start and foolishly hoped that my next round of sleep would be dreamless.

When it was finally time to get ready for school, I was completely exhausted. Dad said nothing when he saw the shadows under my eyes but I could tell he was concerned because he kept stealing glances at me when he thought I wasn't looking. For the first time in years, he offered to drive me to school and I accepted. He must have been looking to give me some reassurance by his presence but it didn't work. I wanted to feel strong and confident about the prospects of the day but I was struggling to stop my hands from shaking. I wasn't sure if it was sleep deprivation or my shot nerves that were to blame but I finally understood why Dad had wanted to keep me from going to school; he was trying to protect me from this. Not the act of actually facing Russ but the fear of the moment when I did. It was too late now.

"Remember what I said Gem, call me the second you feel you need to pull out of this. Even if it is five minutes from now, I'll come and get you."

I hugged Dad tightly, not caring that people could see us where he was parked in front of the school building. I needed a boost to get me through the morning.

The first half of the day went without event. I didn't have any classes with Russ till after lunch and I made sure to avoid any areas where he and his friends would be likely to loiter. I knew my moment of torture would be at lunchtime. I could avoid the encounter by going to the library but there was no point in doing that. I hadn't braved going to school to then spend the whole day postponing the inevitable. If Russ planned to confront me, he would try it in a crowded place so that I wouldn't have a chance to escape. I wondered if he would be surprised that I was making things so easy for him but if he felt that way, his face didn't show it when I walked into the cafeteria and sought him out from the doorway.

As usual, he was sitting with a group of his friends at a table in the centre of the room. He didn't appear to be part of the conversation that was being exchanged at the table; his eyes kept darting around, clearly searching for something. I waited by the door till they rested on me and then I watched as he left his friends without a word and walked towards me. I hadn't expected that. I thought he would wait till I sat down somewhere secluded, that he would try to play it cool, that he wouldn't be so obvious.

A hundred eyes followed him as he approached me, and a few hundred more widened as he stopped only inches away from where I stood and extended his hand towards me. He wanted me to touch him. Right there in the cafeteria, in front of everybody. He knew what that could do and yet it was more important for him to confirm that he wasn't insane.

I stared at his outstretched hand for a moment before I looked up into his face. It was unsmiling yet held no hostility, which hopefully meant that he didn't hate me – yet. He was standing so close that I could see a thin red line across his jaw where he must have cut himself shaving that morning. It was the thought that he had attempted something as banal as shaving that snapped me back into action. Surely, if he was capable of carrying on like nothing had gone wrong in his life, I was capable of pretending that I didn't feel anything abnormal when he held my hand. Holding my breath, I raised my right hand and placed it in his.

Nothing happened. My hand was still in his and I felt nothing at all, only the warmth of his skin. He clearly hadn't felt anything unusual either because he raised his brow in surprise but held on tightly, almost as if he hoped that doing so would bring on a jolt. I was now more confused than ever. What did this mean? Why had nothing happened? I should have been glad at the turn of events but I didn't like not knowing what was going on.

Then I remembered what Dad had said about the Orb being in a transitional state. Was it possible that it really had been the cause of what had happened those first two times? It couldn't be that easy. If it was, then Dad would not have panicked like he had. Perhaps the Orb clearing up yesterday was keeping me from transferring any further visions to Russ but it was not the cause of the problem or the solution to it. I didn't get a chance to ponder much longer because Russ gave my hand a gentle tug and started to lead me out of the room. I could still feel people's eyes on us, trying to figure out what exactly was going on. They probably thought it was the start of some exciting new dysfunctional romance. Tennis champ falls for oddball non-socialite. If only they knew.

I let Russ lead me out of the building and towards the tennis court. It was hard to imagine that it was less than twenty four hours since I had joined those silly sports fans to ogle Russ and his partner as they practised. Less than twenty four hours since Russ's world was turned upside down. Less than twenty four hours since I knew that I was going to leave this place sooner than I expected.

"I always come here when I want to escape the crowd," Russ explained his choice of location as we sat down on the top bench. He still held on to my hand and I didn't have the heart to pull away.

It was weird sitting there with him, knowing that this was the one thing I was told not to do. Even though it seemed we had gone past the freaky jolt phase, I had a feeling so much more could still happen between us. Well, I had promised not to talk to him and so far I had succeeded, Russ had done all the talking. I wondered how long I could hold out for.

"Will you run away if I let go?" Russ asked after about a minute of silence. He had been staring intently at me as I tried to focus on a spot where the tennis net had worn from being hit too many times.

I shook my head but avoided his gaze. I wouldn't have been able to sit there if I acknowledged the desperation in his eyes. He was good at keeping it out of his voice but it had been there yesterday evening and there had been a hint of it back at the cafeteria. When my hand was returned to me, I put it to good use by unwrapping my sandwich. Surely he wouldn't deny me my lunch.

"You're not going to say anything, are you?"

I focused on my sandwich like it was the most important thing in the world.

"Is that because you're not allowed to talk about it?"

From where he sat, it probably looked like BLT had never tasted so good. I was incredibly impressed by his composure. I should have been bombarded with questions once I got to school that morning but somehow he understood that going about things that way would have been ineffective. Maybe he was using the skills of composure and persistence he had mastered over the years as a sportsman to assist him in his real life crisis. Whatever it was, I wished I had some of it.

"Okay, let's try something else. If I tell you what I think is happening, you don't have to speak but you can let me know if I'm on the right track."

I finally looked up at him and nodded. He smiled and I couldn't help returning it. Dad was so going to kill me! I was definitely making things worse but I couldn't see any way out of it. I felt so much more comfortable with Russ now that I knew he knew that I was not quite normal. I was supposed to feel fear and be cautious but for some reason, those emotions weren't building up in me. If he had been hysterical perhaps I would have reflected those feelings too.

"You're a witch."

I actually laughed out loud and carried on chuckling for a good few minutes afterwards. Oh, the silly things people come up with.

Russ wrinkled his nose at me but he carried on smiling. I think he was enjoying the fact that he had finally made me laugh, even though the situation could not be any further from humorous.

"So you're not a witch. Should I just cross off anything that has to do with spells?"

I thought about that for a second before I nodded. I guess I never really liked to consider what we did as sorcery. My views might seem a little naive but spells and potions sting of darkness to me and that's not what we're about.

Russ tilted his head in thought. "You made me change my mind about something I was going to do, but you're not a witch or a sorceress. Guardian angel?"

I'd always liked the idea of that but I knew I was no angel as I was very much as mortal as Russ, so I carried on eating my sandwich in silence.

"You know it would be easier if you just told me."

I shrugged but not with a lot of conviction. I was wondering what the true consequences of telling him the truth would be. He already knew that there was something wrong with me. Normal people don't go around exchanging visions with each other. And they don't run off and hide when confronted about it so I clearly had something to conceal. As far as I was aware, Averters didn't have a secret code that was not meant to be broken. All I had been taught by Dad was to be discreet. Of course I realised that going around telling people what we did would negate the point of our existence. If everyone knew that they had guardians who tried to sway them from making grave decisions, they would probably be a lot less careful about how they lived. It was bad enough that free-will made it impossible for our efforts to be a certainty.

"So is this what that incident at lunch yesterday was about? You got me to talk to that girl so you could do something to her friend. Do you hurt people?"

I couldn't stop an incredulous expression from creeping on to my face. After all I had done to protect them from harm, he was implying I was a danger to them? How dare he suggest such a thing?

"I don't expect you to understand," I lashed out before I could stop myself.

"I could try if you explained it to me," Russ didn't express joy that he had cracked my silence. He just wanted to keep me talking.

"It's complicated," I sighed but I knew the game was over. I had known all along that it was a matter of time before I started talking. What the hell had that jolt done to me? A few weeks ago I would have sworn that I would never ever speak to another person about what I was. Talking to that other Averter hadn't seemed too bad because he already knew what was happening, but talking to Russ? He was cute and nice and athletic and all the other things girls classed as prime rating, but he wasn't one of us.

Even though I didn't talk to the other Averters at school, they were still one up on him because they understood. They knew that we couldn't form lifelong friendships, they knew that we couldn't fall in love and be with anyone we wanted for the rest of our lives. All those things that non-Averters thought were important. All those things I had told myself I didn't want. Now I had gone past contemplating revealing what I was and I was actually going to do it. All because of a metaphysical current that had passed through me to him.

"I would never hurt you. Or Emily for that matter. Not intentionally." I let myself look into his eyes as I spoke. Hopefully he could tell I was being sincere. "But you're right, I did something to you. Only because I had to help you. I don't go around averting everyone's actions..."

"I'm sorry, averting my actions?"

I had forgotten that I hadn't explained that bit to him yet.

"That's what I do. I see your future and I try to convince you to change your mind about your actions. Well, convince isn't quite the right way to put it. It's a bit more forceful than that. I push the thought that would lead to that action out of your mind. Like getting you to stay home that night so that you would avoid something really bad happening."

Russ frowned. "Something like?"

I knew that was all I could reveal to him. How do you tell someone that they would have killed their friends and been badly maimed if you hadn't stopped them from going to a party? "Just something bad. Trust me."

He remained composed as he nodded in acknowledgement. I almost wished he would react hysterically. All this sensible reflection was beginning to worry me. "How is this even possible? Getting into my mind, doing whatever it is you did? If you're not a witch or an angel or a supernatural being, how can you do that? It's not..."

"Normal? Yes I know that Russ, thanks for pointing it out." I cut him off with irritation building in my voice. "I was born with my ability. I can't control it, I can't change it. None of us can. I haven't read any history books that explain it but I know we have existed for a long time." He had to know more than that so I sighed and went on.

"My Dad says we are descendants of a group of Mentalists who lived centuries ago and were used by kings and queens to alter the minds of their adversaries. Most of our ancestors were labelled sorcerers and killed off by those who didn't understand their value. Those that managed to escape the persecution found a way to preserve their bloodline and carried on in secret, using their powers to protect people instead of manipulating them. They formed a pact to atone for misusing their abilities and now we work for no one except those we are entrusted with. I don't expect you to understand any of this but that's the story as I know it. And now you know it too."

Russ stared at me for a few seconds, probably wondering if we both were crazy to be having this conversation. "So what do you get out of it? I'm sure you don't have to do it if you don't want to. Surely you can't be expected to give up your life to protect others for nothing."

I wanted to laugh at him for asking such a ridiculous question but it dawned on me that he had a point. Dad said we were born to do what we did and I had accepted that. What reason did I have to question our motives if we were helping others? But now that Russ had put the thought in my head, I couldn't help wondering why. Honour? Pedantic preservation of tradition? I suddenly felt foolish for never querying Dad more on the subject.

I was aware of the fact that Russ was still waiting for an answer so I mumbled the words, "We need to preserve our bloodline and keep the pact." Those were Dad's words and they sounded hollow to me so I wasn't sure if Russ was convinced by my response.

"Can your Dad do what you do?"

I thought that bit was obvious. "Russ, I've said too much already. The only reason I've told you anything at all is because, for some unfortunate reason, you saw what you saw and I couldn't leave you hanging like that. I couldn't do that to you."

He nodded gravely, his eyes still fixed on me. "Don't worry, your secret is safe with me."

"Is it?" I had to ask. "You don't think it would impress your friends if you told them about this? That you have your very own protector following you around school, making sure that you don't hurt yourself." I was exaggerating what I could achieve but I didn't want to give him the complete truth. I also had no intention of telling him about my lone female Averter status or that we were leaving town in a few weeks.

"You really think I'd do something like that?" The disbelief in his voice made me flush with shame. I hadn't meant to insult him, especially as I could feel the truth oozing from him, but I was finding it more and more difficult to be patient with him when he was so calm. Why the hell wasn't he reacting the way I thought he would?

"I've told you all I can so there is no need for us to sit here any longer." I shoved my empty Tupperware into my bag and stood up.

Russ's hand shot up and grabbed mine before I could dash off. "Gemma, you know this doesn't change anything. I wasn't kidding when I said I'd like us to be friends. Call me crazy but I want to get to know you. I don't care if you're a little different and can get into my head."

I was going to take him up on that and definitely call him crazy. Had I screwed with his mind so badly that he couldn't think straight? I wasn't a little different, I was a lot different and whether or not he understood it, I would have to carry out another Aversion on him in the future if I had a new vision. How could he accept that I could mess with his mind at will and still want to be friends with me?

"Russ...," I began to protest.

"No wait," he interrupted before I could start making my excuses. His grip on my hand tightened and the pressure was strangely soothing. "I know this probably makes no sense to you but I've wanted to speak to you for years and somehow, for the last week or so, I've shared more than words with you. I'm not going to pretend I understand it all but I know what I felt and saw yesterday so I believe you're telling the truth, as crazy as it all sounds. I might need to get my head checked out but I don't believe in coincidences and I'm not going to let you fade into the crowd again."

I had no idea what to say to that. In all our previous conversations, he'd never looked so earnest or sounded so determined and I felt something stir in my chest, just for a brief second. I stopped myself from reaching out to smooth over the furrows on his brow; his handsome face was so badly contorted because of me. Despite all that he knew, he still wanted to befriend me. He really did need his head checked out. It felt cruel for me to pretend to be his friend if it would only last for a few weeks. But another part of me reasoned that we'd come this far so I didn't have much to lose by being nice to him for a little longer. I wouldn't have to reveal much more to him than I had done already.

Besides, how could anyone say no to that face?

"I'll see you tomorrow, Russ." That was all I could manage as I gently prised his fingers off my hand, but a smile crept on to my face and I knew he'd understood that I had just assented to his request because a grin touched his lips.

The rest of the school day went by quickly and I barely noticed the stares I received from people when I walked down the hallway or even when I sat in class. It would probably be days before people stopped talking about the cafeteria episode, especially if Russ kept mute about what had really gone on between us. I had little concern for my non-existent reputation but I didn't want him to suffer any alienation because of me. Having a friend sucked already. I didn't like feeling responsible for someone else in that way.

I decided not to tell Dad about my conversation with Russ but I was going to have to come up with a convincing story about my day. There was no way he would believe that Russ had left me alone. I wondered if he'd believe me if I told him Russ had missed school because he was ill. But then Dad might have thought he was ill because of something I had done to him and that would make things worse. I hated that I was resorting to lies to keep my supposed new friendship with Russ alive but I wasn't sure how else to deal with the situation. For some crazy reason, I trusted that he wouldn't tell anyone about me but what if I cut him off and he took it the wrong way and didn't feel the need to protect me anymore? Surely that was a good reason for lying. I tried to convince myself it wasn't a silly justification as I walked home after school. I was lying to protect us all. Yes, that almost felt better.

I was so caught up in my thoughts that I almost didn't notice the man standing across the street from our house. If I hadn't looked up at the sound of a delivery truck speeding past our usually quiet street, I would have walked into the house and not given much thought to anything outside. But I looked up and saw him standing just outside the fence of No.18, staring intently at my home. He didn't move a muscle when the truck went by as his eyes remained glued to his target. I'm not sure why I decided that the simple act of staring meant he might be a danger to us but I carried on past our house and went all the way to the end of the street until I was sure I was out of his line of sight. Maybe it was the fact that I couldn't sense any vibes coming off him. As far as I knew, the only people Averters couldn't read were other Averters.

So if the burly stranger ogling the lowly house No. 17 was an Averter, why was he there? Did he know who we were? What we were? Dad kept an incredibly low profile amongst others of our kind and we rarely ever had non-Averters calling on us, so a visit from an Averter was cause for concern. Maybe I was overreacting and I should have crossed the street to ask if he was lost or something of that nature. My gut told me I was wise not to have done that so I stood in the corner, hoping I was completely concealed, and I waited.

Nearly an hour passed before Dad showed up in his truck and pulled into his usual roadside spot in front of the house. In that time the man hadn't moved. I was relieved because I thought Dad's presence was a sign that I could leave my hiding place and return to the warmth and comfort of the great indoors but then Dad did something really strange. He didn't go home. Instead he walked over to No. 21 and knocked.

Mrs Burlington was always home, being in her late eighties and confined to TV watching on her couch, so Dad was promptly received by the frail lady that appeared at the door. The stranger didn't appear to acknowledge them because they were not in his line of vision. He was clearly waiting for someone to arrive at our house. I was really confused. Had Dad not noticed him? Had he really come home to answer an emergency call from the old lady or was he hiding next door?

After another half hour wait, I desperately wanted to go home and fill my belly with some food. It was getting a little chilly as well and I was not in the mood to nurse a cold with all my other problems. Just as I was about to emerge from my spot, the man looked around the street, pulled his jacket tightly around himself and walked off in the opposite direction to where I was standing. Just like that. No dramatic exit. He must have had other houses to stare at and we were wasting his time by not returning.

I waited a few minutes before abandoning my hiding place; if he returned and approached me, I would scream for help and Dad would come running. As I started to sprint towards home, I realised that my heart was beating furiously against my chest. I wasn't sure why I was afraid but I was more petrified than I had been when I found out that Russ knew my secret. I was nearly outside Mrs Burlington's when Dad came out and stopped me.

I took one look at my father and knew that he hadn't come back to fix a leaky pipe at the old lady's house. No, he definitely knew what was going on and had taken refuge at No. 21 because he thought that he would be safe there.

"You saw him, didn't you?" Dad asked as he scanned my face for only heaven knows what.

I nodded as I registered the fear in his eyes. I thought I had never seen my Dad so badly shaken up but then I realised I had. That day I returned from school and found him in the kitchen staring into space. He'd said I had nothing to worry about but clearly he had lied.

"I knew I couldn't go home," I could barely recognise my voice. "Who was he, Dad? What's happening? Please don't tell me it's nothing."

Dad sighed and took my hand in his as he started to steer me towards our house. "It's a long story..."

"Isn't it always? Please Dad, tell me who that was and what that was about."

He paused just outside the front door and looked at me. He must have been weighing up just how much to tell me, how much of the information would keep me from screaming and running for the hills.

"Does this have anything to do with whatever happened that day I found you in the kitchen?" I held his gaze, not wanting to give in to his silent plea for me to wait till another day to hear the truth.

Finally, he sighed again and rubbed his temple with his thumb. "That man was Henry Founder, he used to be your mother's Averter, and we've been running from him for the last sixteen years."

SEVEN

I didn't realise my mother had an Averter. That was my first thought after Dad's revelation. Then I shook that thought out of my head because I knew most people had one. I guess it was the shock of hearing my Dad talk about my mother as a real person that rendered me speechless. We never mentioned her in the past. Like every other Averter child, I had no relationship with her except for the months when she had carried me in her womb and nursed me after my birth. I had no idea how she had been selected or who she was or where she was now. Why would her Averter be looking for us?

Then the next thought that came to my mind and perhaps the one that should have struck me first was that I had no idea we had been on the run. Sixteen years? That was more than my entire lifetime. I had been on the run all my life and I had only just found out because some man showed up at my doorstep.

"I thought I saw him the other day in town and I panicked, but then I convinced myself that it couldn't possibly be him. I was foolish to have thought that. He knew

I was at Mrs Burlington's but I don't know if he realised that you had seen him too," Dad carried on as if that explained anything. "We should go in and I'll explain some more."

Some more? He'd better explain everything, I thought as we walked into the house and I followed him to the kitchen where we seemed to have all our serious conversations. I sat on a stool and waited for him to sit beside me but he filled a kettle with water before setting it to boil. Great, we were having a tea break.

"I haven't been completely honest with you," Dad started to say then he stopped and laughed. The sound had no mirth to it, only pain.

I wanted to say something aptly sarcastic like "No kidding" or "You think?"; something that would show my displeasure at the fact that he had been lying to me for such a long time, but I kept quiet and listened to the kettle as it started to hum. I needed something to focus on, other than his face.

"I only did what I did to protect you."

Didn't people realise that saying things like that always made the wait to hear the truth worse?

"Please Dad, just tell me."

Dad came over and sat across from me at the counter. Beads of sweat were forming on his forehead even though the kitchen was cool. The knot in my stomach tightened.

"I was really young when it happened; I lived with your grandfather in a city a long way from here and I was a lot like you when it came to learning about my abilities. I knew all that was expected of me and I was eager to get everything right. I didn't have time for other kids at school because I didn't see the point of mingling with them. Your mother was a girl in my class, beautiful and slightly quirky, just like you've turned out." He stopped at these words and I knew he was thinking about her. "One day she got it into her head that she was interested in finding out more about me so she asked me out."

His story sounded much too similar to mine and I didn't

like it one bit. The most striking part of what he had said so far was that he had known who my mother was. He wasn't supposed to have known her before she was assigned to him. That was not the way things worked. I wasn't comfortable with where I thought his story was going but I had to hear it all.

"I wasn't supposed to fall for her but I did. She was just so…so beautiful and endearing and I couldn't stay away from her. She felt the same way about me so I thought that maybe things would work out for us. I let myself ignore the future I knew I was supposed to have because I was so happy with her. The only problem with our arrangement was her Averter; he had no idea what was going on until it was too late. Because we lived in a city, he had far more people to look out for than in a town like this so he was spread pretty thin, which probably helped us get away with it for a while. Or maybe I was good for your mother at that point so there was nothing in her future calling for us not to be together."

The kettle began to hiss and we both turned to look at the steam that wafted out of its spout. Dad started to get up, as if either of us cared for the tea he was going to make, so I grabbed his hand and pulled him back down. He cast a longing glance at the kettle but carried on speaking.

"We dated in secret for months before he had a vision of what was going to happen. Once I noticed Henry hanging around, I realised who he was and what he was up to. I knew my time with your mother was up but I didn't want to accept it. Whatever he was trying to prevent couldn't be that bad if what we had between us was so good. That was when I did something really stupid."

I almost didn't want to hear it.

"Your mother had no idea what I was even after we left town. I knew she wouldn't believe me if I told her what I was and I didn't want her to think I was crazy. I couldn't tell my father what was going on until we were far away enough from home because I knew he wouldn't understand.

Our kind are not meant to fall in love, we know our role in life and that has never been one of the options open to us. Most Averters see love as an affliction that others suffer from, but the few of us that have loved know it is humanity's one true strength." Dad sighed here. "Unfortunately it was also the downfall of my happiness."

He paused for so long that I thought he wouldn't carry on so I prodded him with a question. "What happened to my mother after you left town?"

"Nothing, at first. She thought we were off on a big adventure to explore the world and do whatever we wanted to do. She'd never had a happy life at home, she fought with her parents whenever they were around to give her the time of day so she sought comfort in others. Even though I had no money, I offered her the one thing she thought she needed. But Henry was right all along because I destroyed her life by making it impossible for her to live the one she was meant to live. I whisked her away so quickly that he didn't even get a chance to try to use his Orb from a distance. She wasn't where she needed to be so that he could carry out the Aversion that would have saved her life. My selfishness ensured that he wouldn't be able to find her."

We sat in silence for a while as I tried to take in what he had just told me.

"How old are you, Dad?" I wasn't sure where the question came from but it needed to be answered. Somehow I knew his answer would be critical to my understanding of the events he had recounted.

I was surprised when my usually coherent father began to shake his head and mutter to himself. "I can't look back now and regret our actions because if we hadn't run off, we would never have had you. You are so very special Gemma, you don't even realise how much…"

"How old are you, Dad?"

I had always taken it for granted that my father was in his mid to late thirties. I had worked it out a long time ago. If he had been assigned my mother when he was twenty one, and she had been lucky enough to conceive me fairly quickly, then he had to be about thirty seven. His answer would be more important than anything he had said to me that evening. Please say thirty seven, I repeated silently to myself as I shut my eyes and waited for what I knew was coming.

"Thirty two."

I needed air. It felt like the room was contracting and the space between my father and I had evaporated. I couldn't see the expression on his face because the room was beginning to spin. The story of my life had been a complete lie and my father was the mastermind of it all. I knew my judgement of him was harsh but at that point all I could think of was how much he had kept from me. How could I tell what was true in all he had told me? Were all his explanations about our abilities false too? The small details he dropped about the lifestyle we were supposed to live, were those all made up?

Dad had made sure we never stayed anywhere for longer than four years. Surely that was another of his attempts to keep Henry from finding us. He knew I wasn't going to befriend any other Averter at school and ask them how things really worked. No wonder we didn't mingle with others of our kind. I would have found out that things were not quite right with the things he had told me.

One key thing his explanation shed some light on was why I had been born female. My mother had not been chosen from the specially selected stock of women like all the others. She'd had no idea what she was getting into. My poor oblivious mother.

The stool crashed to the floor as I jumped to my feet and started to head for the door. I heard the warning note in Dad's voice as he called my name but I didn't look back as I tugged at the door handle and raced out of the house. I didn't catch the words he yelled at me. He was probably worried that Henry had returned and was waiting outside for one of us to emerge but I wasn't thinking about that danger. I just wanted to put as much distance between my father and I before my anger erupted into something I couldn't control. So I did what we Greens did best, I ran.

I wasn't sure where I was going but my body was steering me towards an undisclosed destination so I gave into it. Questioning my subconscious was the least of my worries that evening. I must have been running for almost five minutes before I slowed down to a jog and stopped to catch my breath outside a convenience store a few blocks away from home. That was when I felt the jolt. I almost laughed out loud at the ridiculousness of the situation but the discomfort I felt in the pit of my stomach knocked out any humour that was building up in my system. I looked through the glass at the shop front and honed in on the boy who was serving at the counter. He was planning to rob his boss that night and he was going to get caught. I couldn't see his reason for doing it but I had to stop him. For all I knew, that wouldn't be the first time he would have stolen from the shop but if he got caught, it wasn't just his life that was going to spiral out of control. Something wanted me to prevent that from happening and I had no choice in the matter.

Unfortunately I had left my Orb in my bag when I made my quick exit so I couldn't use it to change his mind from that distance. I took a deep breath and went into the shop. Two minutes and I was out, heading in the direction I had been going before the interruption. Despite my annoyance at everything that I had found out today, I couldn't ignore the fact that I was getting used to this whole mind Aversion business and, shock of all shocks, almost liking it. I felt a sense of accomplishment with every disaster I prevented and it was difficult to prevent a smile from creeping on to my face as I ran towards my unnamed destination. Maybe this was the answer to Russ's question. Maybe all we got out of carrying out Aversions was the rush, the feeling of exhilaration that was coursing through my veins at that moment. Maybe there was no noble cause and we did what we did because we were selfish thrill seekers. The funny thing was I reckoned I could be satisfied with that explanation.

It was only when I got to the junction before Russ's street that I realised where I had been going all along. The stop at the convenience store had not been a coincidence but this was where I had been heading. I slowed down to a walking pace as I approached his house, still unsure why I was there or what I was supposed to do. There was no car in his driveway but there was a light on in a room upstairs. Russ's room. I remembered its location from the night of his Aversion.

My feet stopped under a street light and I waited. I had no idea what I was waiting for but I stood there, trying to catch my breath from my earlier sprint. The only way Russ would know I was there was if he looked out of his window, but what were the odds of that happening? That was probably why I jumped a little when the front door opened and Russ came out. He hadn't turned the light on in the hallway so I had no idea he had noticed me.

"Gemma? What are you doing here? Is everything okay? You're shaking. Are you hurt?" He rushed towards me and grabbed my shoulders with both hands.

Jolt.

I had no clue what he saw when he touched me but Russ's eyes widened in disbelief and he took a step back. Damn it, I thought we had resolved that problem earlier on in the day. He'd even held my hand for a considerable amount of time on the tennis court and nothing had happened. So what had changed now? I wondered if my elevated emotions had anything to do with my ability to transfer visions to him.

"Ask me out on a date."

"Sorry?" That was clearly not what he had expected me to say.

"Ask me out on a date, properly. Like you'd ask out any other girl at school. That's what you really want, right? You don't want to hang out with me every day trying to be friends until you get bored by my presence and move on to the next girl."

The words were coming out fast and I wasn't sure why I was saying them but I realised that was how I truly felt. Despite my better judgement, I, Gemma Green, hopeless Averter of the town of Sandes, liked Russ Tanner. I had just discovered that my entire life story was falsified by my father and yet the one thing I wanted was for Russ to ask me out. Even though I knew there was no future for us and there was no point to this request as this was probably the last time I was ever going to see him again. It was obvious now that I was one hundred percent defective.

"No, I don't," Russ sounded confused but at least he answered honestly.

"So do it, ask me out."

Seconds felt like minutes as I weighed up the idiocy of what I was asking for. Even if, for some unfathomable reason, I was going to stay in town, how was this any different from what my father had done sixteen years ago? He had just told me that we were on the run and that my mother was dead because of his selfish defiance of the rules, yet here I was proving that I hadn't learnt anything.

The funny thing was that my brain kept telling me that this was different. Firstly, I was Russ's Averter so I would see any danger that was heading his way and I would be able to step away from his life if I saw anything catastrophic coming. Surely I was objective enough to be able to do that. The voice in my head didn't sound so confident about that part but I ignored it. Secondly, my mother hadn't known what Dad was and she ultimately had no choice in what had happened to her. Russ knew far more than any of us wanted him to know and he was handling it all remarkably well. Yes, this was definitely different, I tried to convince myself as I waited for Russ to respond.

Once Russ realised that I was dead serious about being asked out, a soft grin crept on to his lips. "I've been waiting to do this for ages and somehow you've managed to take away the zing of it."

I heard myself chuckle. "No one uses the word zing, ever."

"What are you doing?"

"What do you mean?"

"You laughed at something I said. Are you trying to put me off? Or do you think that will make me any more attracted to you than I already am?" Russ teased gently and I felt my face burning with humiliation at the thought that he might be right.

"Are you going to ask me out or..."

I didn't get a chance to finish because at that moment, Russ Tanner closed the gap between us and placed his lips on mine.

EIGHT

I had clearly never been kissed before. I hadn't even practised on the back of my hand in preparation for the glorious moment all young girls dream about. I had always figured there wouldn't be much kissing going on in my life, not with the obligatory mating thing at twenty one all planned out for me, so I had tried not to let myself think about it. Yet here I was, standing in the evening light, being kissed by an exceptionally cute boy I was supposed to keep away from. An incredibly cute boy I realised I really, really liked.

Russ's left hand had somehow settled on the arch of my back and his right hand now cradled the back of my neck. Everything about his touch felt so real, so right, and so safe. I knew I was asking for trouble as I let myself savour the feel of his lips on mine but I couldn't help it. He had awakened the teenage hormones in me I thought would never surface. Annoyingly, at that moment, I started to worry about whether I was doing it right. Russ had plenty of practice; he'd dated Hayley Stern for months last year and I'm sure they got up to more than just holding hands. My goodness, what if he thought I was awful at it? As much as I didn't want the kiss to be over, my mind was racing to places it should have stayed clear of.

Alas, every good thing comes to an end and Russ eventually pulled his head away from mine. I hoped my eyes were twinkling as brightly as his were. I could hardly breathe from excitement with his face so close to mine but I had never been happier. Who knew lips could tingle like that?

"You've never done this before, have you?" he asked softly.

I blanched. I had obviously been right to worry. "Was I that bad?"

Russ chuckled and touched my cheek lightly. "No, you were perfect." Then when I arched my brow, he added with another laugh, "Okay, you were a little bit tense but I know how to fix that."

This time he pulled me close to him and it felt like everything around us melted away as his lips touched mine again. I'm pretty certain that time, it was perfect.

"Gregory's."

"Mmmmmm?" I mumbled when Russ raised his head.

"I'm trying to ask you out on a date. Will you, Gemma Green, meet me tomorrow after school for a good old fashioned date at Gregory's? They have really gimmicky date desserts like double sundaes to share, complete with a glazed cherry on top."

As I heard myself laugh yet again, I realised that I really did want to go on that date and eat that double sundae with him, as tacky as it all sounded. I desperately wanted to have that moment of normalcy with him but I knew better. Dad was waiting at home and if everything he had said was true, this was my farewell to Russ. The hope of something that would never happen. I tried to convince myself that giving him that hope was better than giving him nothing at all.

"Yes, Russ Tanner, I'd love nothing better than to share a gimmicky double sundae with you." And then I detached myself from his embrace and took a step back. "But I have to go now."

Russ still held on to my hand and he didn't let go even when I was a whole arm's length away from him. It was almost like he knew that he was extending our last moment together.

"Don't you want to know what I saw?"

Of course, his vision. I had completely forgotten about that, my head was still spinning from his kiss, his touch. I was turning into a hormonal teenage girl, which to be fair, I was supposed to be. I nodded as he held my gaze.

"You wanted me to kiss you, that's what I saw. Actually, it was weird because I didn't actually see anything this time, I felt it. Like you were telling me what to do."

I wasn't sure what to do with that information. I hadn't even known that I was going to request for him to ask me out or that I wanted him to kiss me until he had kissed me and yet I had passed that information on to him. Dad had some more explaining to do. He had told me that he'd heard of this type of telepathy but he hadn't expanded on it. Today was the day for answers.

I said nothing more to Russ as my hand finally slipped from his and I turned away. I could feel him watching me as I walked to the end of the street and for some reason that made me feel warm and glowy inside. I now understood why it had been a good thing for me to lock away my emotions in the past. All this giddiness was clouding my senses and I needed to be alert for my encounter with Dad. I also had to be on the lookout for Henry. Now that my anger towards Dad had dissolved a little bit, I recalled the warning tone in his voice when I left home and realised I had been foolish not to be more cautious.

All the lights in the house were on when I got home and I wasn't too surprised to see that almost everything we owned had been packed up in the flat pack boxes Dad always kept ready and waiting in the store room under the stairs. He had clearly been busy in the few hours I had been gone. I found him upstairs in his bedroom, folding clothes into a suitcase.

"Tonight or tomorrow?" I asked as I leaned against his open door.

"Tomorrow. It will be a long drive so we need to get some rest." He didn't bother looking up or asking me where I had been.

It was official, we were on the run again but at least this time I knew what was happening. It was funny how being involved in our escape plan made me feel a little bit like I'd aged over the last few hours. There were so many things to consider. Where were we going? How long would we stay there for? How had Henry found us? Would he find us again?

"You did the right thing, Dad."

Dad finally looked up at me and I saw the doubt in his eyes. "You don't really believe that. You don't have to pretend you understand why I did what I did..."

"You did what you thought was best. Am I angry and confused about why you kept me in the dark up until now? Yes. But I can't be mad at you forever, especially if we have to evade Henry. What will he do to us if he comes back?"

I saw that he tried to suppress a shudder but he did a terrible job of it. "There are people who think I deserve to be punished for what I did. I suspect he is alone at the moment but he might go and get backup. Then he'll either carry out what he thinks is fair punishment or he will take me to the others to go through something even more humiliating."

I waited for him to tell me what his punishment would be but he kept quiet.

"Which is?"

"My abilities will be blocked. It's not easy to accomplish but these people can do so much more than you and I could ever imagine. Gemma, I never wanted you to be drawn into that side of our history and I'm sorry this is the way it has come out. I truly am."

I had never considered the possibility of having our powers blocked. Had I ever thought that I would like not to be burdened with the responsibility of my abilities? Yes, of course I had, especially when I was younger and had been anxious about whether or not they would manifest at all. But I had never really thought that my abilities could be forcefully taken away. More so, by people of our kind. I felt my stomach begin to churn as I realised I had to tell Dad the truth about everything. If we were really in as much trouble as he was suggesting, I had to let him know that my abilities were still on the fritz. At least that way he would be able to watch out for me if I accidentally touched a stranger and unconsciously passed our secrets to them.

"It happened again."

For some reason he didn't need to ask what I meant. "With?"

That was the difficult part. "The same boy from school."

"And this has happened only with him?"

I nodded reluctantly, avoiding his eyes. "My Orb also turned orange a few days ago, just before it cleared up." It was best to enlighten him on all my screw ups. The only thing I would keep to myself was what I had shared with Russ that night. Telling Dad that I thought I had feelings for Russ would probably make his head explode.

"Oh, Gemma." I hadn't expected the exasperation in his voice or the dash towards me as I was engulfed in his embrace. I pulled away and tried to read the expression on his face. "I didn't realise I would fail you by trying to protect you from the truth. Maybe I shouldn't have kept so much from you. I was hoping...actually, I don't know what I was hoping for. We have an acute sense of empathy but we are not usually able to project visions to others like you've been doing to that boy."

"Please tell me you're not going to make another grand revelation," I said as my chest contracted. What else could he have kept from me? Had I been born with two heads? Was he keeping the other one locked away in a trunk somewhere dark and secluded?

"All I told you in the past about our Mentalist ancestors

and the culling of our kind is true. What I missed out it that someone, a long time ago, deduced that the best way to preserve our abilities in the purest form was by keeping our blood line male. Female Averters tend to exhibit other abilities which we don't know how to control. When the cull happened, most of the people that were targeted were what we call Progressive Empaths, all female. They were killed because people mistook their powers for sorcery in a time when persecution for heresy and witchcraft was rife. Ever since then, there have only been a handful of female Averters and they have only been born from illegitimate unions like mine. When your mother had you, I didn't feel any disappointment at the fact that you were a girl but I'd never met a female Averter so I thought that maybe if I tried to bring you up the way I had been raised, things would work out okay."

Great, so now I wasn't just an Averter, I was also a Progressive Empath. Whatever that was. I had been told I was different all my life, the only female Averter there was, and now I was being told that I was even more different from different. And I wasn't alone. No wonder the other Averters kids at school didn't like me. My head began to throb at the thought and I winced. Dad must have noticed because he returned to his suitcase.

"I'll explain more on our drive tomorrow; you've had a lot to take in already. But you have to promise me that no one else can know of this. No one."

Who did he think I was going to tell? My imaginary friends? Then I realised that he meant Russ. Why would he think that I would tell him? I hadn't let it slip that I had blabbed about our history so he had no reason to think that I would go off and reveal details of my extra freakishness to him.

"Sure," I tried to sound nonchalant but Dad carried on staring at me.

"You still have time to tell him you're leaving."

Okay, I would officially never win an award for my

acting skills. It was either that or Dad had suddenly developed mind reading abilities.

"No Dad, it's better this way," I whispered as I left his doorway and headed to my room where a suitcase was already waiting to be filled.

NINE

Our new home was in a tiny flat in the town of Springbuck. It was an odd name for a place that had no single springbuck in sight, or for hundreds of miles away for that matter, but we weren't being too picky. To be honest, after we'd been there for four months, I didn't really care about the name of the town or much else about it. The key thing was that it was a long way away from Sandes and had about three times the population so it would be much more difficult for anyone to locate us. The other advantage was that it wasn't so large that it would overwhelm my senses which were still trying to adjust to all the recent changes.

In hindsight, moving to Sandes had been a bad idea but Dad said he had chosen it because he had wanted me to have a semblance of normal life in my formative years. The small population had been ideal for preparing for my first Aversion but it must have been much too easy for Henry to find a female Averter in a town of that size. Despite the fact that I never spoke to the other kids at school, that boy had known what I was and had even spoken to me about Russ's Aversion. We'd actually been lucky that we'd lasted there for that long without word of my existence filtering through to Henry. Female Averters were clearly not as uncommon as Dad had thought because the others would have blabbed to the powers that be if they thought that I was a unique danger to them. Surely if I was that unusual, people would have been queuing up to catch a glimpse of me.

What frustrated me was that now that I knew that there were others like me, I wanted to know all about our advanced empathic abilities but I had no means to extend my knowledge. Dad had called me a Progressive Empath but he didn't know much about my abilities because he hadn't mingled with other Averters since he was sixteen. All he knew about female Averters was the little amount of information his father had imparted on him before he ran away. All rumours.

Our level of empathy was supposed to be so high that we could not only feed thoughts into people's minds but we could transfer our emotions and, if channelled properly, control actions. Which meant that there was the chilling possibility that we could use people like puppets, completely taking over their being. That was what had fuelled the cull. Once the Mentalists worked out that the only people who had these extended abilities were female, the mate selection process was initiated so that only women who had been preconditioned to produce male offspring would be used. I didn't understand the science of it all but it didn't sound like a pleasant process.

Unfortunately that was the extent of Dad's history lesson so for months after we left Sandes, I was subjected to homeschooling on the same boring subjects I'd studied at school. Even though he'd made it sound like he was on top of things, Dad had no clue what he was supposed to do so we had to resort to the internet. A lot. The only reason he thought it was important to carry on with my studies was because I needed a job for later on in life. I couldn't very well go about introducing myself as an Averter when asked my occupation but I also couldn't tie myself to employment that would get me too bugged down with routine. Medicine and banking were out of the question but Dad's handy man job was perfect. The reason he'd chosen that career path was so it was easy for him to pack up and move when he sensed danger. As I had suspected, the four year residence rule had been invented to protect me. Most Averters stayed in one place for most of their lives. It made their lives easier. Dad, on the other hand, had moved us every year for eight years until he made up the four year rule to give me some stability.

The other thing that kept bugging me was my heightened emotions. Before my friendship with Russ, I have never had anything to be jealous about; nothing at all. Not clothes, not money, not boys. But after that night with him, after that unexpected kiss, I kept myself up at night wondering about all the possibilities. What if we had stayed back at Sandes? Would anything real have materialised between us? Would I have gone down the same path Dad had trod? Or would I have waved it all off as foolishness if I had the opportunity to see Russ again in school with all his friends and realised that we were far too different to be companions? What if I glimpsed a future action for Aversion that I didn't want to change? Would I jeopardise his wellbeing for my own selfish desires? That was precisely the reason I hadn't wanted to get attached to anyone at school. Even platonic friendship changed everything.

"Are you alright Gem?" Dad would occasionally ask and I would nod and try to focus on whatever it was I had been doing before my mind had wandered.

Being homeschooled meant I didn't have to go out so much, a thought which gave Dad a lot of comfort but one which didn't ebb my pubescent frustrations. There were only so many books a girl could read before going insane and I'd never been a fan of television so that held no appeal for me. The only time I was allowed out was to help with picking up groceries. Dad didn't want me meeting anyone new or accidentally touching people. Who knew what information I would spread? Avoiding touching everyone I came across was a tough challenge but the few instances this had happened, I had felt no jolts or any other alien sensation.

I began to wonder if Russ was the only one I was able to pass visions to. If so, my abilities were pretty harmless to the world because I was never going to see him again for that to be an issue. It was also a little ironic that my Aversion skills were being confined to these few outings. I had a feeling that Dad only let me go out so that I could exercise my mind bending tricks. I had carried out a grand total of twenty two Aversions in the last few months but I could have done so much more. Granted, one of the Aversions had been preventing a suicide (no small feat) and another had been stopping a teenage girl from abandoning her new born baby on the roadside, but it still didn't feel right that I was cooped up most of the time. Unfortunately I was too cowardly to point out to Dad that running and hiding hadn't stopped my mother from getting hurt. It hadn't stopped any of us from getting hurt.

When the weather became considerably warm, so warm that opening windows and wearing practically nothing did little to stop sweat beads from forming, Dad couldn't prevent me from going on walks around the block to cool off. After so many months of near isolation, I relished the hour I was allocated away from the flat. One good thing about Springbuck was that it was riddled with small parks and playing fields which always seemed to be heaving with people in the evenings. Even better, the chances of me having to carry out an Aversion was much higher when I was within a crowd. My Orb had been working perfectly since we got there and I still enjoyed the rush of knowing that I had changed someone's life with my abilities.

I would probably have carried on like that if I hadn't wandered off to one of the larger playing fields on a particularly scorching evening. Dad and I had struggled with my curriculum that day and he had been in a bad mood when he finally headed off to work so I said nothing to him about my plans to take a longer evening stroll than usual. The urge to extend my walks had been building for days so when I found myself standing outside the Springbuck Sports Centre, I wasn't too surprised that I had strayed even further than I had planned. There weren't too many people at the Centre, probably because using the facilities required payment, but I noticed a group of teenagers nearby dressed in white shorts and tees. Most of them were swinging tennis bags and racquets as they chatted to each other. They looked like they were there for a tournament and from the way they were trying so hard to look interesting and cool, it was probably only day one.

Tennis. I attempted to block out the thoughts that I knew would flood my senses but I failed miserably. My mind quickly filled with images of Russ laughing, Russ frowning, Russ puzzled, Russ walking towards me. Wait, I wasn't imagining it. Russ Tanner was walking towards me, his eyes wide and his lips pressed tightly together. I closed my eyes and shook my head to clear the illusion but when I opened them, he was standing in front of me. Right there outside the Springbuck Sports Centre.

My first instinct was to flee the scene but my feet had developed a mind of their own and remained glued to the spot. Now Russ was staring at me, his mouth slightly open as he clutched a duffel bag which had Springbuck Tennis Juniors Tournament printed on it. Of course, tennis summer season had started.

He'd probably thought that I was a figment of his imagination when he'd seen me initially but now it was clear that I wasn't, his confused expression changed to one of anger. I had only seen him angry once but I could tell that this time he was trying to contain himself. Maybe he was worried that he would scare me off if he showed just how he felt.

"I don't know if Gregory's has a chain here but I'm still up for that date if you are." The steel in his voice was unsettling.

My brain still wasn't prepared to accept that he was there, right in front of me, talking to me like I had only seen him yesterday.

"You don't have to do this, Russ."

"Oh yes I do."

He had been standing a few feet away from me but he crossed the distance between us in a millisecond and stood so close to me that I could see the pores on his face. And those eyes, my goodness, how much sadness they held. I felt worse because I knew I had caused the misery he felt. I took a step back and he closed in but didn't touch me. He had not forgotten the effect touching me had on him. We said nothing for about a minute but it felt like much longer as I tried to think of what to say to him, how to explain what had happened.

"You could have told me you were leaving. I would have understood...or at least tried to understand." There was still an icy edge to his tone but I could tell he was softening a little bit.

I actually snorted as I shook my head like a child who was unwilling to accept what was being said to her. "This is so much bigger than the both of us. It's so much more than I can expect you to handle."

"How will we ever know what I can handle if you don't let me in, Gemma. You can't keep running away from me. Something always brings us together, I don't know what it is but I'm pretty sure we're not supposed to stop it. Please let me in."

And then without warning, he kissed me. Not a gentle kiss like the last time but a hard angry crushing of lips, almost like he wanted me to know how much my disappearance had hurt him. My body tensed in confusion at what was happening. I couldn't understand why he was kissing me; it made no sense that he would want to be associated with any part of my chaotic abnormal life. But he was there and it didn't feel like he was letting go. Just as my body began to respond to the pressure of his lips, I was blinded momentarily by a flash of dazzling light as a jolt passed through me and into his body. Damn it, not again, I thought as I waited for Russ to pull away. But he didn't.

Instead of his usual stunned reaction, he held on tighter and kissed me so deeply that my mind went blank. Completely blank. I couldn't read any other vibes off him, just pure agonising passion. I forgot all about how we had come to be standing outside a park on a late summer's evening in a town far, far away from all that we knew and loved. I didn't even think of the reaction his friends would have to watching him wander off to start kissing a random girl he'd seen on the road. There were probably one or two other people from our school in the group and I didn't consider whether they had recognised me. Most worryingly, I forgot about the importance of whatever it was he might have seen.

"You're running from someone."

"Huh?" I was still trying to catch my breath after he had broken the link between our lips. My foggy mind was slowly unclogging and I began to remember where we were and what we were doing.

"That's what I saw."

That was when I realised what I passed on to him, my fears and desires. The first two jolts we'd shared had been my projection of images of the night of the Aversion because I was so terrified that he remembered what had happened. The one before this had been my surprising longing for him, possibly brought on by the realisation that I had no future with him. This time I was clearly anxious about Henry. Maybe I wasn't just an empath, I was a coward who needed to resolve her problems by inflicting them on others. Well, Russ to be exact. I felt an overwhelming sense of pity for him. He had done nothing to deserve any of this confusion in his life. Despite all my attempts to evade him, he was still being pulled into my life by a force neither of us could understand. It was probably time I started listening to whatever it was the universe was trying to tell me.

"Have that sundae with me and I'll try to explain."

Russ looked a bit stunned by my reply but he recovered quickly and smiled. "You'll tell me everything? I know you don't think I can handle it but it will be so much better for me to know what's happening than for my imagination to keep running wild."

As I nodded, I knew I was being foolish but maybe if I revealed all I could to him, I could make him understand that he was safest away from me. I considered texting Dad to tell him I was still out of the house and might be coming home late but a part of me didn't want to have to explain why. Seeing Russ had nothing to do with Dad or this whole mess with Henry and I desperately wanted to keep the two separate. I needed something to be mine and I wanted that thing to be Russ.

I waited as Russ returned to his tennis friends, gave one of them his bag and made his excuses. The group hadn't stopped staring at us since Russ had come over but he didn't appear to notice any of that, just like he had never cared what people thought back in school when he first started speaking to me. He was much keener on finally finding out what the hell was going on. We started to make our way toward the high street that was round the corner when Russ took my hand in his. My skin warmed at his touch but there was no jolt between us. I hadn't expected one; I had already passed on my anxiety for the moment.

I led him to a busy cafe which looked like it might have good desserts on its menu. To be honest, anywhere would have been fine but I had promised him that sundae and I intended to deliver. It wouldn't be the date I had demanded of him four months ago but I could try to make up for that. Russ smiled at me again and I grinned back. It was a little weird yet nothing we had done felt wrong so I let myself relax. There was no harm in enjoying the moment, especially as I knew it wouldn't last.

That was when I saw him. Henry Founder was standing across the street from us, making no attempt to hide as he stared directly at me. There was no more pretence; he clearly knew who I was. I stopped so abruptly that I yanked at Russ's arm as he carried on walking. It was almost too much for my senses to bear. First, I'd bumped into Russ out of nowhere, and now him? How the hell had he found us? We had been careful not to leave any trace of ourselves wherever we went. Dad and I paid for everything in cash and we had bought cheap non-contract mobiles phones which we only used in emergencies. We were even planning to leave Springbuck in about a month just in case he'd somehow started to track us down. And here he was.

"Russ," my voice was barely audible but Russ heard the sharpness to it and followed my gaze. He paled and I knew that he recognised Henry from the vision. I wanted to hug him right there and then for not knowing the full story and yet not questioning my sanity. My fear of the man across the street was real to him.

"What do you want to do?" He asked in a low voice as we both carried on glaring at Henry.

I had no idea. I'd never really considered what would happen if I ran into Henry, I'd just been focusing on staying hidden and that had worked so far. Even worse, I now had Russ's safety to contend with and the thought that I was putting him in danger had a paralytic effect on my body. But I knew what Dad would want me to do.

"Run." I yelled as I turned and grabbed Russ's hand, pulling him along with me.

The streets were packed so speed was difficult to achieve as we tried not to bump into people who were going about their business as usual. I didn't bother turning to check if Henry was following, I just wanted to put as much distance between us as possible without touching anyone in the process. The great thing about having an athlete beside me was that I had no need to worry about him keeping up.

"This way," Russ said as he suddenly took charge and pulled me away from the crowd into a narrow alley that was filled with empty cardboard boxes from the street shops. I had no idea how he had spotted the slot but I was grateful when we took refuge behind a pile of boxes and saw Henry run past on the street, clearly still in pursuit.

My heart was pounding so strongly that I felt it would burst at any moment. I heard Russ breathing steadily beside me and I almost laughed out at how much better he was at coping with this than I was. But then it hit me. Something was definitely not right with him. Why the hell was he so calm about everything when I wasn't? I was the one supposed to be ready and prepared for all these supernatural eventualities and he was putting me to shame by not freaking out about what I was or about the fact that I was being pursued by Henry. And how had he seen the alley so quickly and known it would be a good place to hide? Come to think of it, what were the odds that he would be participating in a tennis tournament that was being held only a few blocks away from where we were hiding in this town? And minutes after seeing him, Henry showed up. Once I let myself start considering all these angles, doubt took over like a fever and I felt myself shudder.

"Are you alright?" Russ asked. The concern in his voice sounded genuine but I wasn't sure anymore.

I turned to face my object of concern with suspicion etched on my brow but the words that were forming on my lips dissolved as I saw someone coming towards us from behind him. Henry. He must have gone round the block and entered the alley from the other end as I was foolishly revelling in the thought that we had eluded him.

"Run," I yelled again, discarding my worries about Russ's motives for a moment. Until I had time to question him properly, he was still in this mess because of me and I couldn't throw him in with Henry just because I had a bad feeling about his actions and reactions.

We both rose and attempted to make our way out of the alley the same way we had come but there was a woman standing at that end now. It all happened so quickly that I had no time to do anything other than pin Russ to the wall behind me as Henry approached from behind us and the woman moved in too. I had no idea I had the strength to hold a six foot tall teenage boy down but there I was, proving that theory wrong. I had to protect him and nothing else mattered.

The woman moved towards us with lightning speed, hands outstretched and with one index finger pointing towards me and the other at Russ. I had a terrible feeling that it had been a bad idea not to have sent Dad that text I had been thinking about earlier on. That was my last thought before my whole world plummeted into darkness.

TEN

I sensed Russ's presence even before I opened my eyes. He was somewhere to my left and my body turned in that direction as my eyes blinked open. I had to shut them when bright light hit my pupils. It felt like someone was shining a torch directly at me. That was when I tried to sit up and realised that I couldn't move any of my limbs. There were no physical binds restraining me and yet I was immobilised. I forced my eyes open again and saw that Russ was still out cold but he didn't appear to be tied up either.

"You're awake." A female voice stated the obvious. I hadn't realised there were others in the room because all I could sense was Russ's energy. The voice came from my right so I turned towards the speaker. It was the woman I had seen just before I blacked out. She was standing beside Henry, about ten feet away from Russ and I. We were in what appeared to be a large shed, not much bigger than a car garage. It was pretty much bare but our captors had been kind enough to plunk us onto two battered armchairs as they waited for us to wake up.

"Who are you?"

The woman smiled at my question and whispered something to Henry. He didn't seem to like her suggestion because he scowled at me before leaving the room through the only door that I could see. I caught a glimpse of kitchen cabinets in the other room as he exited and I wondered if this was someone's home.

"You'll have to forgive our methods in bringing you here," the woman began to explain as she tucked a lock of her long brown hair behind her ear. There was almost nothing out of place in her appearance; she looked to be in her late twenties and wore a long straight black dress with black pumps and thick framed glasses, no makeup. The only thing that didn't look right was her skin; it looked raw, like it had recently been exposed to a great amount of sun. "Henry is eager to get this over and done with and I promised I would help. My name is Alice."

Was that her attempt at an excuse as to why she was helping Henry hold us hostage? I still couldn't figure out how we were being confined to the chairs but I reckoned they must have paralysed us from the neck down with some form of medication.

"What is he doing here?" I motioned towards Russ with my head.

"We followed him. That's how we found you."

When I carried on staring at her in confusion, she frowned. "You really don't know do you? You're very lucky; your father loves you and did a good thing by trying to train you to be what you are but clearly he didn't do enough. My father didn't even know I existed. My mother raised me without telling me what I was so when my abilities began to manifest, I thought I was insane."

Ah, so she was like me. Funny, I thought that if I ever met another Progressive Empath, I would feel some form of sisterly bond with them. The odds of meeting one was so slim that it was almost unbelievable that she was standing there before me. But nope, I just felt angry. What was she doing helping Henry when he was after Dad and I? Didn't she realise the danger she was putting us in? I considered the fact that she was being forced to assist him but she looked too serene for me to accept that; in fact it kind of felt like she was in charge.

"That doesn't explain anything about Russ." I intensified the steel in my voice as I glared at her.

She nodded and went to stand by Russ, still making sure that she wasn't within either of our grasps. Not like we could try to grab at her if we wanted to. "He is your Sentient Twin."

She'd said that like it was meant to mean something to me but when it became apparent that I still had no clue what she was on about, she rolled her eyes. "You do have a lot to learn," she exhaled before pulling up and sitting on a wooden chair I hadn't noticed before.

"You and your friend here have the curse, or blessing, of finding each other no matter the odds. Your father probably doesn't realise it but this boy is the reason he decided that you should settle in Sandes. The connection is always between one of our kind and one of theirs. We don't know too much about people like you because not many of you exist, but it appears that having a Sentient link is hereditary."

She spoke with so much authority and conviction that there was no doubting she was telling the truth.

"Your father and mother were Sentient Twins too. Your grandfather found his Sentient but was wise enough to stay away; even though he made sure to live in the same town as the woman for many years. Unfortunately your father lacked the same level of self-control and has landed himself in a bit of a dilemma."

She paused to make sure I was taking her words in but I was too shocked to react outwardly. First of all, how the hell did she know so much about my family? Things that I had no knowledge of. And why the hell had Dad not told me that there were more labels for us Mentalists? Averters, Progressive Empaths, Sentient Twins. What next?

Telekinesis? Teleportation? Okay, maybe I was letting my imagination wander a bit too far.

Most of all I felt awful for doubting Russ. There I was suspecting him of being in allegiance to Henry when all he'd done was find me because his body was somehow programmed to do so. They must have known he would eventually seek me out and Henry had waited all this while for nature to take its course. Despite the dire nature of our situation, I suddenly had a glimmer of hope. Did this mean that I wasn't broken? That the reason Russ was so calm about everything, the reason why the Aversion had never fully worked on him was because we had this link? That would explain so much of the confusion that had been building up around us.

I wondered if Dad knew about this Sentient Twin theory. He had not been my mother's Averter so whatever bond he had with her would not have been as problematic as the one I had to deal with. He hadn't told me much about their time together but I'm pretty sure he would have told me if he'd had any supernatural connections with her. Or would he?

Alice went on, not noticing my growing distress. "Most Mentalists don't like it when these connections exist, but there is usually no harm done to anyone so we tend to ignore them. Unfortunately for you, it is rare for Sentient Twins to mate. Those kinds of unions have been banned for a very long time and you, my dear, are a product of such a union. Henry and I found you with a little help from some people back in Sandes and I assure you, others will start to look for you now that they know of your existence."

I had to pretend I was unmoved by what she was saying but I was getting increasingly alarmed. Being a Progressive Empath was dangerous enough and now I was being told that whatever I was could be even more perilous. I had to find a way to get us out of there, to get Russ to safety. Not knowing where we were or what they planned to do to us was a huge disadvantage and I didn't think Alice was going to enlighten me on either of those bits of information.

"So what are we doing now?" I wondered if I could work out an escape strategy from her response. It was all I had to go by.

She glanced at the door and frowned. "Waiting for your father; he should be here any minute. When Henry is through with him, we have to do what needs to be done to end this."

I felt my blood run cold. It began to dawn on me that she was probably the one Dad should be afraid of if he was foolish enough to show up. If only I hadn't waved off calling him earlier on. I wanted to kick myself for my stupidity but I wasn't allowed that luxury. Keep talking, I thought. "And what is that exactly? What could you possibly do to end all this?"

Alice grinned but it was not intended to show amusement. "Don't pretend you don't know." With that she tilted her head and I felt a little lightheaded as the grip that had been on my right hand released. I was so shocked at the realisation that she had been the one holding me down that I didn't think to react like I should have. I was more mesmerised by the fact that the blotchiness of her skin was clearing up as whatever energy she was using to bind us ebbed. But the moment of respite had only been to prove a point and once she put my hand back into a lock, she turned red again.

"If I can bind you and your friend with such ease, you know I can do much worse to your father. He needs to be punished, for Henry's sake." There was a softness to her voice that made me wonder about the nature of her relationship with Henry. She seemed much too concerned about whether or not he gained justice. Surely there had to be something in it for her too.

As if on cue, Henry returned to the room and shook his head at Alice. It looked like he was trying to convey Dad's continued absence to her. Or maybe he was trying to get her to stop talking. But I needed to keep her talking; she seemed to enjoy sharing information with me. Somehow I knew that was our only hope.

"It doesn't seem like it's that easy a task. Your face looks like it will explode if you don't get some air. How much energy will it take to punish my father? I'd say much more than you can manage."

And I meant what I said. There was no way Alice could take away Dad's abilities on her own, not after her little demonstration. Perhaps they were going to take us to others who could carry out the act.

I didn't think her face could get any redder but it did.

"Enough," Henry barked as Alice was about to respond to my comment. That was the first time I had heard him speak and the powerful intensity of his voice made me shudder. When I noticed Alice cower a little, my focus of fear shifted back to Henry.

"Umph," I heard Russ's muffled grunt as he chose that moment to wake up. Henry's booming voice must have had an effect on him. It took Russ a few seconds to realise that he was paralysed and then another few seconds to acknowledge that I was beside him and that we were not alone.

Please don't panic.

I hadn't said the words out loud but Russ's wide eyed glance at me told me he had heard them. He heard them like I had spoken to him when I had carried out his Aversion, except this time I hadn't been trying to push any thought into his head.

I glanced at Alice and Henry to see if they had noticed our silent exchange but their surly expressions hadn't changed.

Can you hear me?

I tried not to move my head as I directed my thoughts at Russ again. He nodded slightly. My goodness, I thought as I tried not to stare at him, what the hell was happening to us? I was struggling to make sense of the situation when all I wanted to do was cry out in frustration. What if this new phenomenon was like the visions which I could only pass on to him when I was highly strung and emotional? Maybe my elevated state of fear was amplifying my connection with Russ so that I didn't need to touch him or push my thoughts into his head with force. Maybe I could use this new connection to our advantage. I didn't want to get too excited at the prospects.

Don't say a word. Pretend you're still out of it.

Russ responded by looking down and saying nothing.

"I really don't see what the problem is," I directed my words at Henry. "My father was young, he made a stupid mistake and the woman he loved died. Don't you think he's suffered enough? Losing her? Running all these years? If you let us go, we can try to make things right. I now know what Russ and I are and what the consequences of us being together will be. Trust me, I do not intend to create a child with him or do anything of that sort." I sensed Russ glance up at me but I went on. "And I'm sure my father will do anything you ask of him but, please, you can't take away his abilities. You'll take away all that he is."

My speech had been an attempt to distract them so that they wouldn't realise Russ and I were having an inaudible conversation but the words that came out of my mouth stunned me with their sincerity. I was willing to give up whatever romantic bond Russ and I had to protect him. Enjoying kissing him was one thing but what next? If we were drawn to each other by a supernatural bond then we'd never had a choice in the matter from the start. I would eventually have felt an attraction to him whether or not I had become his Averter. I knew then that I had been wrong to think that our story could be different from Dad and my mother's. It would all turn out the same.

It didn't look like Henry found any of that useful. He was clearly back in control. "That is not enough. Your friend here will dominate your life, just like your mother possessed your father and robbed him of all common sense. Our abilities are to be shared for all and not reserved for one being." Then, oddly, his expression softened a little as he went on. "You think your father has been protecting you? Whatever he's told you, he's been lying to you. Did he tell you that your real name isn't Green? Your father's name is Paul Colt, not whatever aliases he's been picking up and dropping on the way. And your grandfather passed away a few years ago. Did you know that? Or that your mother's parents never recovered after she ran away and after she died. I'm guessing he mentioned none of that to you."

I had no counter for that. Somehow they knew that Dad had lied to me and was still holding things back from me. But he said he'd done it all to protect me and I believed him. Whatever misguided decisions he had made in the past, he'd never once given me reason to doubt his love for me. Henry was still the enemy and I would be foolish to forget that.

"He's here," Alice's gaze fleeted towards the door and then at me. Her smile re-emerged as we heard the muffled sound of a doorbell ringing. Trust Dad to treat this all like it was a civil visit to a friend's house. Then it occurred to me that he might not know what he was walking into and they could have tricked him into coming there under the pretext that there was a job to be done. It was possible that not much time had passed since they knocked Russ and I out on the street, Dad would still think I was at home. I had to do something, but what?

My theory must have been right because Henry stayed with us as Alice went to let Dad in. He wouldn't know who she was but surely he would be able to tell that she was one of us. He wouldn't be able to read any emotions off her but she must have had something planned.

"Dad," I screamed, just in case he could hear me but I had a feeling they would be prepared for that. Henry smiled at my feeble attempt, walked over to Russ and struck him in the face with the back of his hand. He didn't need to say anything else, I got the message. Tears stung my eyes as I saw blood trickle down the side of Russ's mouth, but he made no sound. Instead he carried on looking at me with a disturbing amount of trust in his eyes. Almost like he thought enduring the pain would pay off at some point. If only I had his faith!

I'm so, so sorry Russ. Dad will be able to help, I just know it.

The words were more to reassure myself than to convince him. I had no idea if Dad had heard me but I had to hope.

The door opened only a minute or so after and Dad walked in holding his Orb in his outstretched open palm and with his face twisted in despair. Alice followed closely behind, a smug smile still on her face as she nodded at Henry and watched as joy erupted onto his face. Sixteen years of his life spent chasing one man and he was finally standing before him, immobilised and exposed. That had to be his crowning moment and we had the luxury of sharing in the pain that would undoubtedly be inflicted on my father. For the first time that day, I felt all hope fade.

ELEVEN

"Put his Orb with the other one," Henry's words were barely audible, as if the splendour of the moment had robbed him of his mighty voice.

Alice grabbed Dad's Orb without hesitation and slipped it into a slit in her dress. I hadn't noticed the slight bulge in her black dress before but Henry must have been referring to my Orb. It had been in my pocket when Alice knocked me out in the alley. I couldn't move my hands to check if it was still there but my jeans pocket looked pretty flat. I wondered why they thought it was essential to take our Orbs away from us. Apart from the weird colour change it had initially experienced, its only use had been to amplify my abilities and help me carry out Aversions from a distance. It wasn't like I was going to try and do that now. Unless...no, there was no way!

I tried to catch Dad's gaze but he hadn't looked at me once since he came into the room. I wanted him to confirm my suspicions but I couldn't get anything off him.

"Dad," I called out, hoping he would turn but he was acting like I wasn't even there. What didn't he want me to see in his eyes? Defeat? Fear? Threads of an escape plan which I wasn't supposed to acknowledge? Maybe he had this all sussed and didn't want me to do anything stupid to wreck his next move.

"You have me now Henry, let the children go. This is not their fight. They don't need to suffer any more for my crimes." Dad sounded so solemn and dejected that I knew there was no escape plan lurking in his head. He had spoken in the same tone he had used on the night he'd wanted us to run. Perhaps he thought this was the only way to give us our freedom but I couldn't believe he was turning himself in just like that. My father, the man who always ran.

Henry's grunt of derision was worse than any words he had said so far. "We are not barbarians, Paul, you should know that by now. The only reason I left you alone those first few years was because I couldn't take her father away from her. She was too young to be without your guidance. Besides, we don't need to hand her in yet. They want her to reach her full potential first."

I felt my eyes widen. They? Who were 'they'? And how did they know I hadn't reached my full potential? Had someone been watching us all this time? Waiting to see if I suddenly morphed into whatever it was they were expecting me to turn into? How was that even possible if Henry had only just found us again? My mind was racing, my eyes darting from Henry to Dad, Russ to Alice. I tried to remain aware of everything that was going on, just in case I was wrong about Dad's intentions and I got a covert signal from him.

"You, on the other hand, broke the law," Henry went on. "And you humiliated me. Do you know how it felt to see her dying in that car crash and not be able to prevent it? Not even be able to try to avert it? You are the worst kind. You think you are better than the rest of us because you felt emotions towards a woman of their kind. Sentiments like that are toxic. You couldn't protect her and now you can't protect her child."

I still couldn't see Dad's face but I could tell that Henry's words were getting to him. His shoulders were hunched and trembling a little and he couldn't look Henry in the eye. I felt Russ turn to me in search of some form of explanation but I couldn't look at him either. Dad's grief was much too powerful for me to be distracted. Even Alice looked like she was struggling with the scene playing out before her. None of us had expected Dad to break down so quickly. I wasn't sure whether I should empathise with him or be annoyed at the fact that he'd shown no strength so far.

"My legs," I'd barely caught the words because Russ had spoken so lowly but once I looked at him, he motioned to his feet. They were moving ever so slightly. My eyes narrowed as I wriggled my toes and felt them move. I had become so engrossed in the unfolding drama that I had almost forgotten about activating an escape plan of my own.

Fortunately Henry and Alice were both caught up in that too because they hadn't noticed that Alice's grip on us was weakening. She clearly wasn't as strong as she thought she was. Holding three of us captive was proving difficult for her. Her skin had turned such a dark shade of red by then that I was surprised she wasn't bleeding out of her pores.

"What other abilities has she been displaying?" Alice pulled the focus of Dad's interrogation back to me. "And don't tell me you don't know, she must have had some teething problems. I could feel the strength of her Orb even before I touched it. She's already gone past Aversions, hasn't she?"

I had been wrong, they didn't know what I was capable of yet but it was evidently important that they should know. And it sounded like my Orb had some part to play in my progression.

Dad remained silent as Henry shoved him for a response. I knew he wasn't one to stay and fight but this was becoming ridiculous. There had to be an explanation for his exceptionally stoic behaviour. I prayed that even though he appeared docile in captivity, he hadn't given up completely and he might have something else up his sleeve. I just wished I knew what.

I felt some more sensation in my legs and realised that my entire lower body would soon be free of Alice's hold. It occurred to me that maybe her grip on us was loosening because she had to apply further pressure on Dad. Maybe he wasn't being submissive, he was using all his willpower to fight her hold on him and move her attention away from us. Did he really think that Russ and I had a chance of getting out of the room even if Alice lost her grip? Henry was almost twice Russ's size and he would stop us easily with physical strength.

I heard Russ whimper as he tried to twist his way out of his invincible bonds. He had been asleep when Alice revealed her power over us so he didn't understand that the only way he could break free was by taking her down. I couldn't imagine how confused he must have felt. Running into me out of the blue, getting chased down and knocked out by a strange man and woman, waking up paralysed and now witnessing what had to be the most bizarre hostage scene in history. I couldn't risk getting him hurt any more than he was already, I just couldn't. He didn't deserve the insanity of our lives even if he really was my Sentient Twin, whatever that implied.

But what if I had been looking at the situation the wrong way round all along? Maybe we didn't need to run, at least not straightaway. If Dad's resistance managed to break Alice's hold on us, I had to be ready to act. What I needed was a way to block Alice's abilities and disarm Henry at the same time. If what I had sensed about Alice's feelings for Henry earlier on was correct, maybe I could use that to our advantage. I didn't have access to the many tricks she had developed over the years but I had a connection with Russ's mind that they were unaware of and that was a pretty good weapon to wield. The only problem was that I had a feeling I needed my Orb back to achieve what I had in mind. They had taken it away from me for a reason.

Russ, I need your help if we're going to get out of here in one piece. Please trust me on this. Whatever I tell you to do, just do it.

A raised brow was his only sign of doubt before he nodded and listened to my ad hoc plan.

"I know what else she can do."

No one had expected Russ to speak. As far as they were concerned, he was only there as an incentive to get Dad and I to behave. Even Dad turned around at the sound of his voice, disbelief apparent on his face. I wished there was a way I could convey my plan to him but I'd never been able to communicate with him without words.

Alice was the first to react as she walked towards Russ. Remember how I said we could tell if someone was being dishonest? It was a terrible ability to share with my adversaries. I could tell she was trying to read him. I felt the binding on my waist release as I noticed Russ's legs stiffen. With her attention on him, she'd increased her hold over him.

"And why would you want to tell us what you know?"

"So you can let us go. Please, I can tell you what she's done."

"No Russ, don't," I yelled in my most distraught sounding voice. I hoped I sounded convincing as I pretended to try to twist myself free. I had never been so relieved that Averters couldn't read other Averters. "She'll never let us go."

"I have to try, Gemma." Russ's acting skills were much better than mine but I'd told him that lies would not fool them so he knew not to go too far.

"You have my word." Henry spoke from his guarding post beside Dad. The way he looked down at my father, I knew he would never be thrown in as part of the deal. "We'll let you two go if you tell us the truth."

"And her father?" Russ didn't know the gravity of Dad's crimes so he still thought he had a chance.

Both Henry and Alice snorted at this and I winced. "He knows his fate. He'll be released when we're done with him."

"Russ…" I pleaded again.

"She can pass on visions to me when we touch. She's done it a few times. I see what has happened, what she's thinking, what she's afraid of."

The room went silent as we waited for the revelation to sink in.

"And?"

"And nothing. That's it."

"That's it? Visions? Only when you touch? You want us to release you for that?" Alice rolled her eyes in frustration then she turned her attention to me. "How are you doing this? How are you blocking his lies from me? I know he's lying, that can't be it. Your Orb has more energy in it than that. Much more. Tell me how you're doing this."

I hadn't expected her to doubt him and I certainly hadn't wanted her to turn her attention back to me. I felt my body begin to go tense again as she started to approach my chair and I knew we were losing our window of opportunity. I had to do something fast but I had no idea what.

Dad's unexpected scream sent a chill through the room. It was the sound of a man in excruciating pain, the sound of a man who needed to break free or die trying. We all turned to look at him and I saw my father staggering towards Henry, Alice's hold on him was still in place but he was pushing past it with all his might. I felt my body free up completely as Alice focused all her energy on him. Somehow Dad must have figured out what I had been attempting and was giving me the distraction I sought. I stared at him for a few more seconds, mesmerised by the thought of what he was doing, until the sight of blood flowing from his nose and ears jarred me to action.

Alice had backed us to concentrate on Dad so taking her down was much easier than I anticipated as I jumped off the armchair and threw myself at her. I didn't flinch at the crunching sound of skull hitting ground. I felt Russ jump up and rush past us to Dad's aid as Henry moved into action to restrain him. That hadn't been part of my briefing to him but I was grateful for his foresight, Dad needed him more than I did at that moment. I had to trust that both of them would be an even match for Henry's large frame, especially now that Alice had lost all control over us. But I also knew we didn't have much time before she composed herself.

My hand went straight for her pocket as I retrieved the two Orbs she had been hiding. I couldn't sense the force she said she had felt from my Orb but I prayed that she had been right about its magnified energy. I just wished I knew what the hell I was supposed to do with the damn thing now that I had it back. I had hoped that I wouldn't need to do much to wield its power once I held it in my hands but I felt nothing.

"Gemma, watch out," Russ called out to me just before I felt a blow to my stomach. Alice was still lying on the floor beside me but she had mustered enough strength in her body to try to prevent me from rising. As I doubled over, blinded by pain, I wondered why she wasn't trying to bind me again with her mind. Perhaps with the knock to her head, she couldn't channel her powers the way she had done before. I felt her struggling to sit up and failing. I could also hear scuffling and grunts from the other end of the room as the men carried on their struggle with Henry.

"You can't use it here. If you try, you'll hurt someone." Alice's breathy words surprised me. Did she really believe that I knew how to use my Orb in some exceptional way other than to avert minds? If I did, surely I would have already tried using it to end the pain that we were all causing each other.

I was about to tell her that she was overestimating my abilities when I heard something crash into a wall. I looked up and saw Dad sprawled on the ground, his chest was rising and falling but he didn't look like he had much fight left in him. Russ was still standing but looked almost as defeated as Dad did, with his shirt ripped down the front and smeared with blood. I had no idea whose blood it was but there was a lot of it everywhere. Henry stood solid before them, no sign of fatigue showed on his beefy frame. What kind of animal were they battling? Was his rage so extreme that it had given him superhuman strength? There was no way Russ was going to defeat him on his own when he had that glint in his eyes.

A soft groan from Alice shifted my attention back to the woman and I saw that her eyes were fixed on Henry. Her breathing was laboured and her pupils were dilated but she kept her gaze on him. Her skin had lost its red glow when I'd rammed myself into her earlier on but I could see the colour slowly returning. I suddenly realised why she wasn't attempting to bind me any longer. She was weak but she was using what little strength she had to help Henry. In some way she was fuelling him to be able to overpower an athletic youth and a handyman in his prime.

I had initially been impressed by her ability to bind us because I hadn't realised an Averter could have control over other Averters the way she had done. Binding us would have entailed tapping into the part of our brains that controlled movement; this would have been fairly easy to accomplish if you knew what to do. But making an Averter physically stronger? That surpassed everything I had thought us capable of.

Once I recovered from the shock of what she was capable of achieving, it became clear what I had to do in turn. Or at least what I had to try to do.

I turned and punched Alice in the side, so that she wouldn't try to stop me, before I lifted myself off the ground and lunged at Russ. None of them had been expecting my movement so by the time I grabbed on to Russ and passed on a vision to him, it was too late.

You will start to forget every word I say even as I speak...

"No", I heard Alice scream as my Orb turned a soft orange hue. I hadn't expected the glow or the heat it was emitting but I held on tightly and tried to tune out her voice. It wasn't possible that she could have heard what Russ and I were saying to Henry but she must have sensed it. We had to keep going. Our lives depended on it.

There is no need to panic. Nobody in this room is a threat to you. Paul Colt is not your enemy. You will leave this place and return to where you came from. You will stop your pursuit of us and you will have no recollection of our existence from now on.

I wanted to add more but I didn't want to push my luck. After all, that was all we needed, for Henry to leave us in peace. If this worked, what more could I ask for? I held my breath as we watched Henry's ferocious expression ease into a puzzled stare. His gaze shifted from my face to Russ's and then to Dad's body on the floor but his confused frown didn't lift. It was only when his eyes found Alice that recognition crept back on to his face. Then he went over to where she lay and sat down beside her, cradling her head in his large hands as she sobbed away.

TWELVE

For a second I thought we might have done more than just avert him. It felt like we had switched off a light in him, perhaps turned his brain into mush. I hadn't averted a lot of people's thoughts in my lifetime but of the few Aversions I had carried out, nobody had exhibited such a strong reaction to my words. Not just my words, mine and Russ's. This would never have worked if I hadn't channelled the connection I had with him, the one Alice had been raving about earlier on. I knew my abilities weren't stable enough for me to wield with such intensity and precision but with Russ, I had been able to control them. I had been able to avert an Averter.

I was still holding on to Russ but I probably didn't need to anymore. He'd done what I'd asked him to do and it appeared to have had the desired effect but I didn't want to let go. The warmth of his hands on mine gave me far too much comfort for logic to apply. He must have sensed my frazzled emotions because he squeezed my hand reassuringly at that moment.

"What's wrong? Why is he so quiet?" Dad had finally

pushed himself up against a wall. He looked like he had gone through a wrestling match with a grizzly bear but he almost sounded like himself again. I couldn't believe he was asking Alice to clarify the situation but there was no one else we could ask.

Alice's laughter was humourless as it came between her sobs. I felt a little tug of guilt as Henry silently moved her hair away from her face. There was far too much affection in his action for there to be no deeper link between the two of them.

"She took away the one thing that has driven his life for nearly two decades and you're asking what's wrong?" Alice laughed again and held Henry's other hand. "He doesn't understand why he's here at all. You know, he was young too when you ran off with that girl and what you did wrecked him. It might seem irrational that he pursued you for so long but her death haunted him and he believed the only way to purge that demon was by punishing you. I guess I should be happy he will have no recollection of any of it now; he is finally free to be who he could have been. You do realise that you've done the same thing he was going to do to you, don't you? You've taken away what made him who he is."

I hadn't even thought about that. I had only been trying to protect us. He was going to hurt my father and my friend, what else was I supposed to have done?

"I didn't realise...I was only trying to...it's not the same thing. He still has his abilities. You were going to take away Dad's." I began to protest.

I didn't want to hear her explanation anymore. Her words were building up more guilt in me and I didn't think I could face it. The thought of shutting her up gripped me and I wondered if we could avert her too. If it had worked on Henry, maybe it could work on her.

"That won't work on me." Alice had sensed what I was thinking. I didn't think she could read my mind but she clearly had an advanced sense of perception. "Henry didn't have the ability to block you but I do. We don't need to hurt each other anymore."

I believed her but I didn't lower the Orb or let go of Russ's hand. Even if we couldn't avert her thoughts, maybe we could achieve something else against her. Anything to stop her from retaliating for what we had done to her friend.

"Don't worry," she sighed, "I'm not going to try to bind you when I'm so weak. Not when you've just discovered such an unstable source of power." When I glanced down at my Orb, she shook her head and motioned towards Russ. "I'm impressed. I've never met an Averter who has been able to push thoughts out of another Averter's mind. How did you know that would work?"

I was completely thrown by the fact that she knew I had used Russ for the Aversion; his lips had not moved and he could have only been standing beside me for moral support as I had averted Henry. But she knew better. I had to supress the surge of admiration I felt for her. I couldn't let myself wonder how my life would have turned out if I had grown up living with someone like her and not Dad. Someone who knew about the complex potentials of my existence. Someone much more similar to me than Dad could ever be. But then I remembered that I was still different from her. She had made it clear that I was a specimen for observation and the only reason she wasn't harming me was because a group of other Mentalists had told her not to.

I wasn't sure if I should reveal any more to her but Dad and Russ were also looking at me for an explanation. "You said Russ and I are twins of a sort and we have a telepathic connection so I wondered if my actions would have more of an impact if I tried to combine the energy that links us. I wasn't sure it would work but after I saw how you were helping Henry, I had to try something. Aversions are the only mind tricks I know how to carry out."

Russ looked baffled by my statement, he had been knocked out when Alice revealed our Sentient Twin link so nothing I had said made any sense to him. I'd have to explain later. Dad didn't look too shocked so I wondered if he already knew the reason behind his ill-fated link with my mother and the fact that it was a hereditary trait. Maybe that was why he didn't feel so guilty about his selfish actions that resulted in my mother's death.

"What are you going to do now?" Alice asked in a solemn tone. Henry had stopped touching her and the frown on his face showed that his mind was returning to a place of confusion.

I shrugged and looked at Dad. We couldn't just let her go, could we? She would surely come after us once she regained her strength. But I didn't know what else we could do to stop her.

"You have to leave us alone and take Henry with you." It was Dad who spoke. He had found the strength to rise to his feet and he came to stand beside us. He appeared to be serious about his request.

Alice smiled. "You know I can't do that. It's not just about Henry anymore. She clearly needs help. She can't survive this on her own and you're of no more use to her. I can be there for her..."

"No," Dad barked so fiercely that Russ and I jumped a little. I'd never seen him that mad before. Ever. "You think I'd let you and Henry take my child? After all he's done to us? After all you tried to do tonight? You think I'd let you teach her all your mind games? She's fine with me, she's always been fine with me."

"Clearly not," Alice scoffed. "Look at how clueless she is about what she can do. She has no idea. You have no idea. Even if I don't help her develop her abilities, they will still manifest and she'll be in real trouble then. When they realise her potential, they will come for her. They might not make a move immediately but before she is out of her teens, they will come for her. You did the unthinkable and created a Sentient from a Sentient and she might have gone unnoticed for longer if Henry's obsession with you hadn't brought her to their attention. You can't change any of that so let me help her."

This mystery 'they' again. I didn't like the sound of whoever 'they' were especially as Dad paled when Alice spoke about them. But I didn't want to sound ignorant of their existence in front of her; she already thought I was naive enough as it was, so I reserved my questions for later. Dad owed me an explanation if nothing else.

"Please just leave us." Dad pleaded and we could all hear the desperation in his voice.

Alice appeared to consider this for a while before she stood up slowly, leaning on Henry for support. "Fine, if I can't change your mind, we'll go. But you know I can't leave him in this state. I have to try and restore some of his memory, there was too much of you wrapped around his life for him to ever be the same again if he doesn't remember you. And when he finally does remember, we'll come looking for you and you'll wish you had accepted my offer."

I understood that there was nothing more to be said between us when Dad took my elbow and began to steer Russ and I towards the door. We backed out of the room and into the kitchen I had glimpsed earlier on. Neither of our previous captors made any attempt to stop us but we remained cautious even after we went through the kitchen door and out towards Dad's truck. The small bungalow we had been in was perched at the top of a hill on the outskirts of town. Henry and Alice had probably rented the place because there was no other residence close by, which explained why no one had reacted to the sounds of our scuffle.

We piled into the truck and Dad asked Russ for the address where he was staying. He received a mumbled response about the tennis team lodging at a hostel on the other side of town and we set off back to civilisation. Just before we pulled out of the driveway, I noticed Alice had recovered enough to stand and watch our departure from one of the windows. I could have sworn I saw a smile light up her face. Why would she smile at a time like this? There was nothing joyful about the way things had ended, especially for them. I said nothing to Dad but the frown on my face must have been deep because Russ squeezed my hand and attempted a smile.

I had completely forgotten that I still clutched the Orb and Russ's hand but now I clearly didn't need either of them so I let go and slipped the Orb into my pocket. It felt a little like Russ hadn't wanted to let go but his face didn't give anything away so I thought maybe I had imagined the hesitation. Even if I had wanted to maintain physical contact with him, it felt too weird with Dad sitting beside us. For a group of people who had just gone through a traumatising and possibly life changing experience, we were eerily quiet for the half hour drive across town. It was only when we pulled up outside the multi-storey building Russ was staying at that we jumped into action.

"Thanks for the lift, Mr Green," Russ's words felt silly and out of place but I didn't think he knew what else to say.

"You can't mention any of this to anyone," Dad's response was barely audible but he held Russ's gaze and my friend nodded quickly. I could tell Dad was weighing up if we could trust him.

"Not a word. I promise."

And we both knew he meant it. Besides, who would believe him if he told them?

"I'll see him off," I informed Dad as I hopped out of the car with Russ without waiting for permission. This was it, my final goodbye to him. I thought I had crossed that bridge back at Sandes but I was going to have to do it all over again. I felt my heart drop to the bottom of my stomach as I followed Russ into the hostel's lobby where Dad couldn't see us. The place was buzzing with kids of all ages, mostly chaperoned by fed up looking adults who couldn't understand how they had given up their summer to hang around rowdy under aged people. At first no one noticed us as we paused a little way into the room, but then people started to cast puzzled glances at Russ. I looked down at his blood smeared ripped shirt and grimaced. What a sight we must have looked.

"I told you we had an extraordinary connection," Russ broke the silence with a grin. As usual he seemed not to notice anyone else in the room but me. "I'd felt it for such a long time but I couldn't put it into words. It got even more unbearable after that night you stopped me from getting into the car."

He paused for my response but I remained silent.

"Did I really just help you push thoughts into a man's mind?"

I had to smile at that. "Yeah, you did. Crazy, right?"

"Insane," Russ beamed back. "I still don't understand most of what's happened so far, especially tonight."

"I'm not sure I do either but I plan to figure it all out," I admitted. "I'm sorry for dragging you into all this, Russ. We didn't have much choice in what happened to us, if we really believe Alice's Sentient Twin story, but I could have been stronger and not gone to your house that night before Dad and I left Sandes. Maybe we would have been able to stay friends, but now...everything's changed."

Russ looked both annoyed and puzzled. "You don't really think any of this is your fault, do you? Gemma, crazy twin theory or not, I like you and I think you like me too. We'll never know if we'd have felt the same way if you weren't a you-know-what and I wasn't your first...whatever I am, but I have a feeling I'd have liked you anyway. I always wondered why you didn't appreciate the effect you had on people when you walked into a room but now I know you've just been stuck in your head trying not to get close to anyone. Whatever else has happened, I am happy I've had a chance to be a part of your life."

He touched my cheek lightly and I felt my head tilt towards his palm as my eyes closed. I wanted to believe what he had said, that the bond I felt with him was not only because of what we were. I wanted to believe that I genuinely liked him for who he was but I wasn't sure anymore. If Dad had been so gripped by the connection he had with my mother that he'd acted so foolishly, how could I trust anything I felt?

Russ must have misread my silence because he withdrew his hand and resorted to joking. "Sentient Twins, huh? Does that mean I shouldn't have kissed you? There is something not right about kissing your twin. Sounds a little bit incestuous if you ask me..."

He looked pretty shocked when I cut him off by reaching up to kiss him. Deeply. It felt nothing like the first two times we had kissed and those had been pretty intense. Maybe it was because I was the one that instigated the action this time and I knew exactly what I wanted to get out of it.

When Russ lifted his head from mine, I saw the uncertainty in his eyes. "I think I'm beginning to recognize your goodbyes."

"I don't think we have a choice."

"I know. You have to figure out things first."

We stood there for a little while, heads close together, soaking in the moment.

"Will I ever see you again?"

I shrugged without looking at him. He wasn't aware of Alice's theory of us finding each other no matter what distance we put between us but it was probably best to keep it that way. I didn't want him to spend the rest of his life wondering if he had unwittingly relocated himself to a place near me, even if he never got to see me again.

"I have to go. Dad's waiting," I said as I took a step away from him. I didn't want our parting to be drawn out. My heart couldn't bear it.

Russ must have understood because he didn't try to stop me even though the look in his eyes said he wanted to. I could have kissed him then for being so level-headed but that would have made the situation even more difficult. My subconscious hadn't transmitted any jolts to him when we touched so I took that as confirmation that our business was done. That was what I needed to propel me out of the door.

When I returned to the car, I made sure not to sit facing forward so that Dad wouldn't see my tears but I was certain he knew I had lost control of my emotions. We said nothing to each other on the drive home, even though I wanted to start grilling him about all that we had encountered that evening. My mind needed the break. But when we got home and Dad's first move was to start locating boxes for packing up our stuff, I lost it.

"Are you kidding me? Is this all we ever do? Run? When were you going to tell me about these other people Alice mentioned?"

Dad put down the box he held and turned to face me. "I was hoping we could avoid this conversation completely but evidently I was wrong."

He was kidding, right?

"I don't want to run anymore," I said with an intensity I hadn't realised I possessed.

"I don't want you to run anymore either," Dad admitted but the tone he spoke in suggested something else. "I should have shown you this before." He pulled out his wallet, extracted a crumpled passport sized photograph and handed it to me. The woman in the photograph was beautiful; there was no other word to describe her, just beautiful. Her skin appeared to glow despite the fact that the rest of the photo paper had dulled considerably over the years. And there was a vivacity in her eyes that told me Dad must have had no chance trying to fight off her advances.

"Is this..."

"Yes."

I looked nothing like the woman who was supposed to have been my mother but I could see why Dad had fallen for her. There was something about her image that gripped me. I'd never felt any affiliation with her and yet I now wanted to know everything about her; all this from an old photograph.

"Why now? Why didn't you show this to me months ago when I found out about you two?"

Dad sighed as he tucked the picture back into his wallet. "Because Henry was right. I was selfish and I didn't want to lose you too, Gemma."

"I don't understand."

"I want you to go back to Sandes..."

"What?" He had to be joking. Or maybe he'd hit his head too hard when Henry had thrown him against the wall.

"Listen to me carefully. I want you to go back there and I want you to live with Mrs. Burlington's for a while, at least until you finish school and you can get a job of your own. You have to push the thought into her head, just as if you are carrying out an Aversion on her. You have to make her believe that she is your guardian and that I am off somewhere far away making money to support you. It should be easy for you to do now that we've seen what you're capable of. I will send money for your upkeep and I might even be able to call you every now and then but I can't stay with you. You will be safe there; they have no reason to hurt you. If you remain discreet and carry on doing what you've been trained to do, they won't do anything to you."

"Wait, Dad, stop!"

I yelled the words because I didn't know how else to express my disbelief at what he was saying. Yes, I now knew that there were other Mentalists out there who had some interest in us but Henry was the one he was running from and Henry was no longer a threat. Why would he think it was okay to leave me on my own in Sandes? It made no sense.

"I tried to keep you with me, pretending it was for your safety, but the truth is I didn't want to be alone. Especially so soon after I lost your mother. But things have changed and you're all grown now. This is the only way we might have a chance to be together again in the future. All Alice has to do now is look for Russ to find you and I'm sure she will turn up the heat now that you've screwed up Henry's mind. The others will help her find you if they already have an agreement with Henry about punishing me."

"But Dad, who are these people? You still haven't said why we have to worry about them?" That had been all I wanted to know before and it felt even more crucial now.

Dad motioned for me to sit down for this part of the story. "There are always people within factions who think they have authority over others of their kind. People who feel they need to maintain order or we will live in a world where everyone runs around doing whatever they want. Our kind are no different. These Mentalists are descendants of the ones who took control after the original cull. I think their intentions are honourable but from the little I have heard about them, their methods of achieving the order they seek are not so clean. My father told me about them when I was a boy but we had no reason to worry because we weren't planning on doing anything wrong."

"But then you met my mother."

He nodded . "My father moved us to the town she lived in because he was secretly following a woman; at least he thought it was a secret. But we must have also gone there because I was meant to meet your mother. I didn't know we could have Sentient Twins until afterwards but it explained a lot. I didn't show you her picture because I didn't want us to talk about the relationship I had with her. I didn't want to discuss the possibility that the possessive feelings your grandfather and I had were passed to you."

"If you think having a Sentient Twin is so bad, why do you want me to stay with Russ?"

Dad sighed and shook his head. "Gemma, I don't know why we have these connections when others don't but we can't run from it. We must have them for a reason and even though I might have handled mine badly, you don't have to go down that route because you're much more sensible than I ever was at your age. My actions resulted in your mother's death but you are the outcome of that union and I have a feeling that there is a greater purpose to your existence. Running from Russ won't help him because he will keep trying to find you and they know this. If you stay with me, you'll put him in a bad position and if I return to Sandes, I'll make it too easy for Henry to find me when Alice helps him recover."

"The others want to know if your abilities will be a risk or a bonus to their authority so they won't bother you just yet but they'll want to be able to monitor you. They are a powerful group and we shouldn't take their interest in you lightly. If you return to Sandes you won't be on the run and you might be able to live a better life than what I can give you at the moment."

"Dad, Alice said I need help. She said I can't survive this on my own."

Dad shook his head furiously. "You have all the help you need within yourself. Look how you handled Henry back there. I didn't teach you that. I can't teach you how to wield what you have but I don't think we want someone like Alice to teach you either."

I tried to stay calm as I thought about this for a while. He was asking for a lot but I couldn't dispute his logic. If I left Russ behind, I would effectively turn him into a stalker and he wouldn't even know it. He would never live a normal life because of me. From the sounds of it, my grandfather got it right by hanging around but never communicating with his Sentient. That part was too late for us but I could still make things easy for him in some way. The real sacrifice here was that I would lose my Dad. I wasn't sure how long he thought he needed to keep away from me but if we were waiting for the Mentalists to make a move first, who knew how long that would be?

"You told me never to avert anyone for selfish reasons."

"After what you've seen tonight can't you tell that I've said a lot of things over the years that haven't been true? Gemma, this is bigger than everything I've tried to teach you in the past. The connections we have can't just be coincidences. Maybe I found your mother so that I could have you and maybe you have to stay with Russ for some other reason. Only time will tell but if you come with me, you'll never know."

He sounded pretty convinced by his words and I knew I had no choice in the matter. I was going back to Sandes for Russ's sake.

"So I head to Sandes to pretend nothing has changed and you go off into the sunset."

Dad's smile didn't have much life in it but he reached out and gave me one of those hugs that always made me feel that everything would be alright. "We don't have to do that just yet. You can stay with me for the rest of the summer; we can travel around the country and I will teach you everything I know. No more lies. I'll even tell you all about your mother and grandfather and we can pretend we're a regular family for once."

I couldn't stop the smile that tugged at the corner of my lips. Up until recently, I had never cared about my mother or grandfather and yet I was excited at the prospects of learning more about them. Maybe getting a glimpse into their lives would give me clearer insight about myself. Maybe what I needed to help me control my feelings for Russ was hearing how Dad had dealt with his feelings for my mother. Things were definitely changing in the Green household.

"I'd like that," I said quietly. "But let's not kid ourselves, there's nothing regular about the Greens."

"Colt. Sorry about that one, it was unavoidable." Dad had the good grace to look remorseful.

"Colt," I tested the name out for myself. It sounded too weird for me to accept but I was going to have to get used to it, amongst other things.

It was going to be a long summer.

THIRTEEN

My name is Gemma Colt and I am a Progressive Empath. It doesn't sound as kickass as being an Averter but, trust me, it is way cooler. A lot has changed in my life in the last six months. I've sort of lost my Dad, who was all I had ever known, and I gained a Sentient Twin, Russ. He's kind of my only friend too and even though we are drawn together by powers that we cannot control, we can't be together in the way we want to because there is a danger I will become obsessed with him.

Russ thought he'd seen the last of me after the incident with Henry and Alice so when I showed up on the first day of school at Sandes, his stunned reaction was expected. He'd been standing with his usual group of friends and he broke away from them and staggered towards me as I walked right up to them. I had never been so forward in public before but things were going to be different this year. If I wanted to be a part of his life, I was going to have to make an effort. All for his protection, of course.

"I hear Gregory's serve a pretty good double sundae."

I could feel a hundred eyes on us as everyone in the

hallway wondered what the hell was happening. Was Gemma Green (ehem, Colt) really asking Russ Tanner out on a date in full view of other people? And hadn't she mysteriously disappeared from town at the end of last term?

To his credit, Russ recovered pretty quickly and I could have sworn his eyes twinkled as he gazed into mine. Then he reached out and took my hand in his. This time I saw what it was I passed on to him and we both smiled. It was good to know that words weren't always needed between us.

"Want to meet my friends?"

I cringed a little but I forced myself to grin back. Sacrifices had to be made for the greater good. "No better time than the present."

"By the way, there's a big guy watching us pretty closely. He seems more shocked than everyone else that you're back." Russ leaned in to me and whispered.

I had already found out the name of the Averter who told me I messed up Russ's Aversion all those many months ago, Peter Foist. Dad said I had to watch out for the eyes of the Mentalists back here. They only knew about us because of what other people reported back to them. Something told me Peter Foist did not have my best interest at heart and I had every plan of staying one step ahead of him.

"We have a lot to talk about," I whispered back to Russ as I steered him towards the baffled looking group of teenagers he'd stepped away.

Clearly Sandes is not the safest place for me to be but nowhere really is at the moment because of what I am. And nowhere will be until I understand why the Mentalists are interested in me. So I'll stay here until Dad comes back to get me or until I figure out how to get the Mentalists off my back on my own. But I have Russ, so maybe it won't be as painful as it sounds. Maybe we'll figure out why out of all the people in the world, we are Sentient Twins.

On second thoughts, don't hold your breath.

Coming Soon
SENTIENT
Book Two of the Mentalist Series

If you enjoyed *AVERSION*, you may also like these other works by Kenechi Udogu

The Other Slipper

When Jo finds a lone glass slipper on the night of the royal ball, she realises that there is more to the seemingly ordinary object than meets the eye. Searching for its owner, she is led to the palace where the princess sets her on a journey that thrusts her into an unexpected world of magic and illusions. It soon becomes clear that there is a lot more to her mission as she discovers startling secrets about her past and struggles to embrace her destiny.

The Altercation of Vira

The people of Vira have long awaited the arrival of their lost princess, Elve. Legend has foretold a season of great change in the dawn of her return. For the Maracans, she brings the promise of fortified control over their rival kindred. For the Cefans, a glimmer of hope in an existence filled with oppression.

The only problem is their princess is eighteen year old Ama Brown, an ordinary girl living an ordinary life, who has no idea that she is about to be drawn into a world where an age old battle is brewing and nothing is quite as it seems.

The Summer of Brian

When Charlene Bowman's parents take on a teenage houseguest for a month, she doesn't expect much to change for her that summer. But Brian arrives early on a Saturday morning, handsome and confident, throwing Charlene's world into turmoil. Discovering he has a girlfriend, Charlene tries to appear sophisticated and makes up a nonexistent boyfriend. Too embarrassed to tell him the truth afterwards, she consults her best friend Orla who suggests they find a candidate to play the part. A search ensues and hope is found in Nathan, a boy in their year, who appears to need their help as much as they need his. Could Charlene be about to learn a lesson in life and love?

You can connect with Kenechi via Twitter @kenechiudogu
On her Facebook Author page at
www.facebook.com/KenechiUdogu
Or on her blog at
http://caeblogs.wordpress.com

Printed in Great Britain
by Amazon

61262864R00080